Also by K. M. Walton

crackєd

empty

K. M. WALTON

Simon Pulse

NEW YORK   LONDON   TORONTO   SYDNEY   NEW DELHI

SIMON PULSE

An imprint of Simon & Schuster Children's Publishing Division

1230 Avenue of the Americas, New York, NY 10020

First Simon Pulse hardcover edition January 2013

SIMON PULSE and colophon are registered
trademarks of Simon & Schuster, Inc.

For information about special discounts for bulk purchases,
please contact Simon & Schuster Special Sales at
1-866-506-1949 or business@simonandschuster.com.

The Simon & Schuster Speakers Bureau can bring authors to your live event.
For more information or to book an event contact
the Simon & Schuster Speakers Bureau at 1-866-248-3049
or visit our website at www.simonspeakers.com.

Designed by Mike Rosamilia

The text of this book was set in Adobe Garamond Pro.

Manufactured in the United States of America

2 4 6 8 10 9 7 5 3 1

Library of Congress Cataloging-in-Publication Data

Walton, K. M. (Kathleen M.)

Empty / K. M. Walton. — 1st Simon Pulse hardcover ed.

p. cm.

Summary: Deeply depressed after her father cheated on and divorced her mother,
seventeen-year-old Adele has gained over seventy pounds and is being bullied and abused at
school—to the point of being raped and accused of being the aggressor.

ISBN 978-1-4424-5359-3

[1. Obesity—Fiction. 2. High schools—Fiction. 3. Schools—Fiction. 4. Self-esteem—Fiction.
5. Family problems—Fiction. 6. Emotional problems—Fiction. 7. Rape—Fiction.] I. Title.

PZ7.W1755Emp 2013

[Fic]—dc23

2012011562

ISBN 978-1-4424-5360-9 (eBook)

To my husband, Todd:

Thank you for believing in me from day one—

which was 9,472 days ago. I love you, for always.

Maybe I Have Disappeared

I LIKE THE IDEA OF MAKING THINGS DISAPPEAR.
It's something I've been thinking about a lot lately.

It's the dead of night, the murky time that's thick with shadows and mystery, and I'm watching David Blaine and Criss Angel YouTube videos on my phone. As usual, I'm completely blown away. It all looks so real. I stare at the ceiling for a while, and my phone goes dark. In the blackness I listen to the steady hum of traffic. I lie still as stone and think.

The people's reactions to the magic are the best. They're always freaked out—questioning, smiling, looking to their friends for explanations that never come. It's one of my favorite moments.

My little sister coughs from her crib across the room and startles me. I close my eyes and start fantasizing about making out with David or Criss. They're both delicious.

I roll my eyes in the dark. Neither of them would touch me, not since I've put all of this weight on. Fantasy ruined. I put my phone on my nightstand. I toss and turn, trying to get comfortable. There are things I'd like to vanish from my life—maybe even a person or two. I'm not talking about killing anyone, but having them gone would be sweet.

I fluff my pillow and pull the blankets up around my face. I've already watched (and rewatched) a ton of videos tonight. I need to fall asleep. My opening game is tomorrow.

I'm in the locker room, yawning as I get into my jersey. It took some concentrated online searching to get one in my size. You try Googling "plus-size softball uniform" and see what you come up with. Answer? Nothing. The company that made the rest of my team's uniforms only went up to a sixteen, which was fine for me last season, but I've managed to gain seventy pounds since last summer. And the royal blue on my uniform is a slightly brighter blue than the rest of the team's.

Should make for an interesting season.

I know the only reason coach kept me this year is because

K. M. Walton

I'm a hitter. Even as I gained weight all last season I was still the best hitter on the team.

"Listen up!" Coach booms. Everyone takes a seat. "East has Forman pitching today, so watch her slider." Coach Douglas goes on and gives her pep talk, and we end it with our chant. I don't feel like chanting because I'm so damn tired.

Our hands are all stacked on top of one another. Everyone's hyping themselves up, and I'm wincing as I evaluate the thickness of my forearm compared to my thin teammates'. Mine is easily double the width.

"Come on, Dell! Let's hear it!" Coach shouts.

I snap out of it and join in. My stomach clenches after each word, but I lay it on thick. I turn my head slowly from side to side—I want them all to know how psyched I am—and I chant like a banshee. Our shortstop, Amy, shoves me with her shoulder, her face curled in a snarl. "I'm gonna need to hear out there. Could you not scream in my ear? Thanks."

I smile and nod. "Sorry, lost my damn mind there for a second." I growl a few times to get *her* to smile. "I'm pumped, Amy! *Rawr!*"

Amy smirks. "Ha-ha," she deadpans.

I look around as the huddle breaks apart, and no one catches my eye. They're all talking and bantering among themselves as they make their way out of the locker room. Not one girl looks back to see if I'm coming or where I am. I'm by myself. Maybe *I* have disappeared.

Coach's head is suddenly in the doorway. "Let's go, Dell! Wake up."

I snap out of my stupid thoughts and grab my hat and glove. As my feet hit the grass, I hear the tail end of the crowd cheering. I squint into the blazing sun and pull my hat down onto my forehead so I can see. Both sets of bleachers are full, since it's our first game. I make my way to the dugout and notice people lining the fence along the first- and third-base lines. Lots of kids are here today, which is unusual. Typically it's just some parents and a few teachers who love to watch softball.

I take my seat on the bench and immediately spot Cara— top row, left corner, like always. My gaze drifts a few rows down to my father's usual spot. I know he's not there. I still hoped he would be. Even though my father has been a jerk, I always liked when he showed up for my games. He hasn't been to a game in a long time. His girlfriend, Donna, doesn't like the sun.

Before my father cheated on my mom and blew up our lives, I was proud of him. Proud of his brainiac job, and proud of the kind of dad he was. He's the one who got me into softball. He told me I was a natural. He even coached my team

K. M. Walton

when I was little. The man documented every team I played on and every big moment with pictures and videos. Before each season he and I would sit and watch some of my best hits or slides or catches, and he'd give me pointers. He didn't take the photos and videos when he moved out. Instead he leapt off the diving board and landed in the selfish pool.

Then he tried to drown the rest of us in it.

As Coach gives her last-minute pointers, I zone out, staring at the cluster of guys standing next to the bleachers on our side.

I spot Brandon Levitt right away.

I've been crushing on him hard since middle school. Whenever I see his smile and the way he bites his lower lip, it makes my knees buckle.

It takes me just a split second to realize that Brandon's group is actually our baseball team with their coaches. Our teams try and support each other as much as we can throughout the season. A group of wandering girls suddenly grabs the attention of the baseball team. There's lots of movement as boys high-five each other and girls fling their hair, jumping, hugging. And then there's a kiss.

Brandon and his girlfriend, Taryn, lock lips. A surge of nervous energy goes directly to my heart.

I want to be kissing Brandon, which, as with the Criss

Angel/David Blaine scenarios, I understand is a complete impossibility, given the fact that I am not popular, not pretty, and fat. Not the combination to attract the gorgeous star baseball pitcher with the hot body and big blue eyes. I may be a dreamer, but I am not an idiot.

Luckily, the game starts, and I refocus my attention. I play right-center field, and I think I've used my sleeve to mop off my face eight hundred times out here. We're in the top of the seventh. As of yet I haven't had a hit, which is unlike me. I think it's this heat.

We're losing, one–nothing.

East doesn't score, and now it's our turn to bat. I head off the field into the dugout. To shade. Glorious, glorious shade. The baseball team and their girl-crew have planted themselves along the first-base-line fence. They're lined up twenty long. I'm going to have to run by them if I get a hit. My face crumples into a squinty scowl as I register this hideous fact.

Amy catches my expression and says, "You can't give up, Dell. We can win. Just stop making faces and hit the ball."

I give her an over-the-top salute and a goofy grin. She shakes her head and then says, "It's not funny," over her shoulder as she walks away.

I can't win with her today. I don't have any more energy to try to break the tension with my comedic genius. If Amy only knew how close I am to passing out, she'd be up my ass even more.

By the time I guzzle two water bottles, we've managed to get two outs. I grab my batting helmet. I'm on deck. I do a few practice swings and watch our current hitter get a single. I am now the winning run.

Please, please, please don't let me look stupid running the baseline. Please.

I take a few deep breaths. I should be able to do this. I've done it a bunch of times. I used to be so sure of myself as I stepped into the batter's box. Not anymore—each pound I've gained has jabbed at my confidence. The 286th pound must've been particularly pointy and sharp, because I feel deflated. And to make matters worse, I got zero sleep last night.

I step into the batter's box and get into position.

"Hit it over the fence, Dell!" comes from my right. I don't look over, but I'm pretty sure it was Brandon. I swallow hard and lick my lips. At least he's not mooing.

The ball is released and I make contact. I toss my bat and run.

First base suddenly zooms away from me like in a cartoon. I feel like I'm running underwater. With bricks tied to my ankles.

The shortstop picks up the hop and throws it to first base. I'm out.

I still run through the bag. My heart is pounding when I come to a stop. I desperately want to put my hands on my knees and catch my breath, but I can't because it'd be too obvious that I'm about to pass out. I don't want Brandon to see me panting—actually, I don't want anyone to see me heaving. I put my hands on my lower back and raise my eyes to the sky, hoping to open up my throat and let air in.

"Why are you even out here?" East's first-base player shouts over her shoulder as she runs off the field.

I haven't caught my breath yet so I can't answer her. *What do you care,* I think to myself, wiping off my face. The East team has left the field. My team has left the dugout. I am alone out here. I drop my eyes and shake my head.

What was that, Adele? Huh? What the hell was that?

Right now would be the perfect time to be zapped invisible, because I can't stand here forever. I have to walk off the field, but I'm trapped—the only way off is past everyone leaning on the fence. They're all still there, goofing around.

Showtime.

I shout, "Hey!" The group turns my way. I form a pistol with my hand and pretend to shoot myself in the temple. I go big with an exaggerated head snap and stagger. "Right?!"

I hear some light laughter roll through the crowd, and then everyone breaks apart. Kids walk away in twos and threes. Taryn's laugh slices the air. She's still surrounded by a few people—Sydney, Melissa, Emma, Brandon, and his buddy Chase.

And Cara.

I hadn't seen her over there when I did my little fake-suicide-funny-ha-ha show.

Taryn looks over their heads, right at me, and says loudly, "She's too freaking huge to hustle! She should *not* be running. Anywhere."

Laughter.

My breath catches in my lungs and I gasp for air. I may pass out right there on first base, in front of them all. I don't have a funny retort for Taryn. In fact, I am mortified into silence. Taryn turns on her heels and walks away. Her groupies all follow, except for Cara. She waves, points to where we always meet, and then scurries away. Why is Cara with those girls?

I somehow get myself together and walk off the field as fast as I can. My thighs rub together with each step. By the time I reach the locker-room door, my skin stings so badly I swear there should be blood seeping through my stupid polyester uniform.

I lean against the wall and inhale the smell of sweat. I don't want to go in there. My teammates are quiet. I close my eyes and picture them all moping around.

I toy with the idea of just leaving, walking home and not looking back. I don't care about my T-shirt and jeans in my locker. Then I remember my backpack. I have homework.

Shit. I have to go in there.

Coach is addressing the team with her back to me as I enter the locker room. Everyone watches as I waddle toward the back wall, trying not to let my thighs touch in any way. I'm sure I look like I've just crapped my pants. I catch two eye rolls and one sneer. *Thanks, bitches.*

"Everyone has a bad game, ladies. Even the pros. We let this one get away. Let's remind ourselves how badly we want States this year," Coach says. She drops her voice down an octave. "Don't ever stop wanting it." Her eyes match the passion in her voice. "When we stop wanting it, we lose. It's that simple. Is everyone with me?"

My team gives her a weak "Yeah." I don't even open my mouth.

"Do you want to win?" Coach shouts.

"Yeah!" the girls shout. The energy in the room lifts.

"Do you want to win States?" Coach asks again.

Coach's passion is contagious. Something feels awakened inside of me. My organs quiver. They've been switched from off to on. I'm alive again. I join in this time. "Yeah!"

I want to win a state championship. I always have. Coach's words have done their job. I'm officially inspired. My guilt from today's shitty performance slowly melts away as I pack up my stuff. Winning matters to me again. I want to feel the surge of pride that comes with hard work and success. How could I have let myself fall apart like this?

My hands work with silent enthusiasm, changing clothes and packing up. I'm done before everyone else. I sit back and watch my team in various stages of undress and marvel at their smallness. Don't get me wrong—they're definitely not a girly-girl group. Our best pitcher could probably level half the baseball team with her eyes closed, and she's less than half my size. Some girls have their legs up on the bench, untying their cleats. I couldn't get my leg up on this bench anymore with a crane.

But not for long. Good-bye pizza, ice cream, and cheese fries. I want to win.

Coach suddenly materializes in front of me and tells me we need to talk. I know what's coming. Diet talk. But I'm ready to hear it this time. I leave my stuff and follow her back to her office. She closes the door, walks behind her desk, and sits down. I give her a little smile, just to let her know I'm on her side. She's stone-faced and motions for me to sit down with her head.

"You looked awful out there today, Dell."

I tighten my mouth and nod.

"I wanted to give you a shot this year because of your past performances. You've always been our best hitter."

I squint. This isn't heading where I thought it would. Exercise, eating right, blah, blah, blah. Why am I sweating again? My face, if wrung out, could fill a juice glass.

She reaches across her desk and hands me a towel. "I should've done this preseason. I'm sorry, but this isn't going to work." She exhales. "You're not in shape, and that's not fair to the rest of the team. Do you understand?"

I look through her as I lie and say, "Yeah." I think I'm about to get cut.

"I wish I didn't have to do this, Dell. But, Christ, I can't have you blowing our chances at winning state. I have to cut you. Take the weight off, and we'll talk next season."

"Yeah," I repeat. I look away and stare at the Phillies calendar thumbtacked to the otherwise blank white wall.

Softball scholarship to college—poof.

Degree in communications—poof.

ESPN sportscaster job—poof.

The only things connecting me to my shithead father—poof.

Now that's some fucking magic.

Coach doesn't say another word, and neither do I. Like a

K. M. Walton

lost kid at the mall, I wander into the locker room with wide eyes and terror in my heart. The rest of the team is gone. I lean against the cinder block wall and smack the back of my head against it a few times. Despite my size, it never occurred to me that I could get cut from the team. I walk over to my stuff, grab my bat, and grip it until my knuckles turn white. I want to smash it into the wall again and again, until I've reduced it to a pile of dust.

"Turn off the lights on your way out, Dell!" Coach shouts from her office.

My hands release a little, and I start nodding for some reason. With shaking hands and a bobbing head, I somehow get the bat into my bag. Now I can't bash up the locker room. I just want to get out of here. Far away.

I know Cara is outside waiting for me, yet I walk around the front of the building to avoid her. I am not capable of talking to her right now. She's probably hanging out with the popular kids anyway.

On my walk home, my brain goes on processing overload. By the time I reach the steps to my apartment I've come to two major conclusions:

1. I've never meshed with my team socially. They've never invited me places or included me in stuff.

I've always been detached, even freshman year
when I was skinny. The weight I've put on has
definitely pushed them further away from me.

2. Truthfully, I never needed any of those girls in my
   life—I've always had Cara. They can all, including
   my coach, shove softball up their firm asses.

Lots and Lots of Food

THE NEXT MORNING CARA FALLS IN STRIDE WITH me as we walk across the back field to school. My jeans, in all of their cotton-breathing glory, feel like heaven on my thighs compared to the hideous softball pants, and I'm walking fairly normally again.

"Hey, Dell." Cara nudges me with her shoulder. "Happy Friday."

I pull my earbuds out. "Yeah, Friday."

"You didn't answer my last text. You totally fell asleep, didn't you?"

After I got home yesterday Cara and I had a three-hour

text session about the softball bullshit. At first she was all pissy about me ditching her after the game, but eventually she calmed down once I told her why.

She stops walking and puts her hands on her hips. "You ungrateful wench," she teases. "I would never have fallen asleep."

I blow right by her with a grin. "Get over it."

I can't tell her that I hadn't fallen asleep or that I'd stared at her last text until my eyes watered. My fingers had just refused to respond to her message—I guess because I had no good answer.

I hear her quicken her pace, and we fall back in stride. "Seriously, Dell, why *didn't* you just tell your coach you'd go on a diet?"

I shrug. I still have no answer to her question. Why didn't I fight to stay on the team? I mean, out of the tons of stuff I *wanted* to make disappear, softball was never included.

Cara shakes her head. "I don't get it. You haven't even tried to lose the weight."

"Just drop it."

"You sound so mad. Dell, come on. You can't be angry. Sports are all about winning. I mean, I completely understand why she cut you."

Isn't that nice? My best friend *completely understands why*.

K. M. Walton

Dreams of my future have shriveled into tiny bits of pain. The rest of my walk to school I pretend each pebble I kick is one of my dried-up dreams. It ends up being stupidly unsatisfying because the pebbles are too small. I need stones—solid and strong enough to break windows. My withered-pebble dreams are useless. Empty and weak.

Like me.

In a blatant attempt to change the subject, Cara says, "Did you do Zuckerman's homework? The man is a sadist. Who gives seventeen-year-olds eighty-five trig proofs to do in one night? He's sick."

I tuck my hair behind my ear. I want to tell Cara that I don't care about the homework, Mr. Z., or anything really. I want to tell her how dark it is inside my heart after getting cut from softball. How I couldn't sleep. How coach's words looped in my brain for hours, haunting me all night long.

But I don't say anything. Cara's not good with emotional stuff. She sort of shuts down or changes the subject instead. She'd probably abandon our friendship if she knew how fragile I feel right now, and then I'd have no one. So I keep my sadness to myself. It's private and it's all mine.

I nod and fake it. "I did the homework. For three freaking hours. Z-man *is* a hater. Period. End of story. Good night. The end."

"Yeah, after we stopped texting, my night sucked too," Cara sympathizes.

I quietly exhale and look straight ahead at the kids congregating on the sidewalk. I don't think Cara knows the meaning of "sucked." Her parents are together, she still lives in our old neighborhood, weighs the same as she did last year, has long blond hair, big blue eyes, and decent boobs. She is a genuinely confident and happy person. Despite the fact that I ballooned to the size of a baby elephant after my father left my family, Cara, for reasons unknown, remains my best friend.

Lately, I think Cara just tolerates me, which sucks because we've been best friends for almost half of my life. I wish we could go back to the way it used to be. We went on our first roller coaster together. Got our periods the same summer. In eighth grade, we analyzed our first kisses for months. They happened mere weeks apart, and all we talked about was how we wanted the boys to kiss us for longer than two seconds, preferably with some tongue action. I cried with Cara when her cat got feline leukemia and had to be put to sleep. I painted the freaking headstone, which sits below her bedroom window.

I want to go back to when we laughed at anything and everything. Like freshman year, when the weird gray color of the school's taco meat made us laugh so hard that we snorted root beer all over our lunch trays. We don't do stuff like that anymore.

Cara has no idea my crush on Brandon is in full swing these days. I've kept that to myself. I like it that way. If I told her, she would no doubt remind me of the obvious: Brandon is going out with Taryn Anderson. Which would really mean: If he's dating Taryn, the most beautiful girl in our junior class, there's no way he would date you, Dell. Get real.

So how I feel about Brandon remains my secret.

Cara and I make our way to our spot and sit side-by-side on the brick wall. Since it's spring, practically the whole school's out here waiting for the first bell. I glance over at Cara.

She smiles. "What?"

"Nothing." I wonder if Cara can really see me. I blink a few times, and she turns away. I follow her gaze to the Taryn and Brandon crew. I probably weigh the same as three of those girls combined. They're all thin and skinny-jeaned, with shiny straight hair. The guys wear baseball hats, T-shirts, and long, baggy basketball shorts and have killer bodies.

I join Cara in her blatant staring, and after a while I see something I've never noticed before—this group does a lot of touching. Holy shit. If they're not hugging, they're high-fiving or linking arms or shoulder-shoving or head-nuzzling. The girls touch the girls. The boys touch the boys. The girls touch the boys. And the boys definitely touch the girls. Everyone's touching. All. The. Time.

I've seen enough of these beautiful people feeling each other up, and I study Cara's face. Her raised eyebrows and slight grin paint her mug with blatant yearning. Lately, Cara's been bringing up our social status during our walks to school. She wants us to break into that group somehow. She wants us to get invited to their parties.

I think I'm holding her back. Her funny, overweight sidekick seems to be repelling instead of attracting popularity. I get it.

I decide Cara can't see me. Not the real me. Not past who I show to the world. I'm the first one to make fun of myself, the goofball who doesn't fight back. Believe me, I can put on a decent show.

Deflection—I've perfected the art.

If I laugh first, then no one is laughing *at* me. We're all laughing together. Most of the time, stuffing myself with this phony sense of happiness does an okay job of protecting my heart.

God, no wonder Cara can't see me. I'm so padded with jolly bullshit that I could probably survive a ten-story fall. Hell, I'd probably bounce on the sidewalk.

I wasn't always like this. I didn't always wonder if people

could "see" the real me and shit. I used to be a size ten and only eat when I was hungry. Then my dad left, and I fell apart. I hate the label "daddy's girl" because it sounds all pink and glittery and wimpy, which I'm not. But I was definitely a daddy's girl. My dad and I were tight. I always went to him instead of my mom—for Band-Aids, homework questions, friend advice.

Now I blame him for everything.

I don't know, I mean, tons of kids have parents who split up. They don't eat themselves into a size twenty-four. But my father left a hole when he moved out, and this hole needed filling. I filled it with food. Lots and lots of food.

The first time I ate what my mother described as an "obscene amount of food," I leaned back in my chair as this deep feeling of comfort overwhelmed me—it was so real, like an actual thing. I felt peaceful. Full. Whole. Then after a few minutes my stomach cramped up and I had to lie down.

Cara has abandoned her aching stare and is watching a video on her phone. Then a loud *moo* comes from somewhere in "the group." I look up with pinched eyebrows. It's louder this time. Brandon waddles over to us, his arms out to the side, puffing out his cheeks. He comes to a stop, like, three feet from us, and smiles that smile. "Come on, Dell, do it!"

Cara shoulder-shoves me playfully and grins. "Come on."

I know what I have to do. Time to deflect.

I stand up, toss my backpack on the ground, and get into my stance. Squatting down like a sumo wrestler, I rest my forearms on my thighs. "You want it?" I tease, soothing the crowd so they don't attack first.

Brandon nods. At a quick glance, it looks like maybe eight or ten guys followed him over. Nearly our entire baseball team. Taryn and her girls are off to my left. They're watching, but obviously not wanting to be too close to the spectacle.

The morning sun beats down, and beads of sweat form above my lip. I want to crawl into a cool, dark cave and never be found. Instead, I'm about to pretend I'm a sumo wrestler for a bunch of guys.

I force a smile and give Brandon and his friends what they want: I moo. Loudly. Immediately the guys burst into hoots and cheers, high-fiving one another and me.

Brandon can barely speak. "Th-that was your best one, Dell!" He bites his lip and holds his hand out at me for another high five. Our hands smack together, skin-on-skin, and I wish I had the guts to look him in the eye.

The guys walk away, back to their usual place on the sidewalk. I'm left standing there, the happy fat girl.

"Wow, you do that so well," Taryn deadpans. She reaches up and smoothes down her long black hair. It looks like she's petting herself. Emma, Melissa, and Sydney stand behind her, nodding in agreement. Everyone's smiling at me like they're in a beauty pageant or are robots stuck in uberhappy mode.

"I guess it's because I'm part sumo wrestler and part cow," I say. "You should've seen my old house at Thanksgiving—half of my family wore white diapers, and the other half chewed the lawn out front. It's one of my favorite memories."

They all laugh. Even Cara.

As I join in, I watch their faces, Cara's in particular. Her eyes are bright and full of life. She's laughing so hard, she reaches over and grabs Sydney's arm to steady herself. Her volume reaches a root-beer-snorting level, and my eyes well up. None of the girls look at me. They're having a moment *together*. Even though I'm standing right there with them, I'm not included. I can tell.

With a chorus of "ahhhhs" they compose themselves. I wipe away my tears and give a few exaggerated exhales as if I, too, have laughed so hard I've cried. The girls form a circle, and I am mostly out of it. Actually, just my shoulder is included. I make no attempt to insert myself, because if I did, I'd have to shove Sydney and Cara out of the way.

Taryn strokes her hair again and looks at me. "I love Thanksgiving, because of the food." She grins, tilting her head to the side. Those are some well-practiced bitch moves. She licks her lips and eyes me up head to toe. "You understand what I'm saying. Right, Dell?"

My backpack suddenly feels so heavy. It presses on my shoulder with absoluteness, and my knees give a little. I break eye contact with Taryn, swinging my backpack around and setting it at my feet. They all look at me expectantly. With a straight face I say, "Food is everything to me. I want to marry food and have food babies and a food pet."

This gets everyone going again. The rise and fall of their laughter mixes with the din of morning—hissing buses, slamming car doors, the murmur of half-awake teenagers, and my pounding heart.

Taryn says to everyone but me, "So, who saw that picture of Ronnie on Facebook? She looks like a whore."

Emma's and Sydney's eyes bulge and they exchange an uncomfortable giggle at Taryn's comment. Melissa says, "I did. Ever since she got boobs, she's had them hanging out in every freaking picture. Get over yourself, Boobie."

They laugh. They nod. They make no attempt to widen the circle to let the rest of me in. Cara is definitely part of the circle. If she could radiate happiness, she'd be the damn sun right now.

The first bell's piercing buzz fills the air. From across the way Brandon calls out, "Taryn, you have any gum?"

K. M. Walton

She skip-walks away, taunting, "Why, do you want a kisssssss?" The other girls turn and follow their leader. Cara stays put, but I can see the longing on her face. She watches them walk away, and her eyebrows lift slightly. I'm waiting for her to bite her lip, to throw her arms out and shout, "Don't leave me!"

She likes that my mooing brings us attention. I wish that she'd tell me not to do it. Plead with me to have some self-respect. The last time I slept over at her house she made me moo for her. She wet her pants. We never get too deep about stuff. It's just how our friendship works.

I scoop up my backpack and start walking. "Coming, Cara?" She's still frozen in place. She suddenly reanimates and smiles.

I want to tell her how the tears I just wiped away were real and how it hurt me that she didn't make room for me in that circle. But I know that would make her uncomfortable, and I'd probably cry again, so I change the subject. "You playing the piano in the talent show this year?"

Cara nods. "You should try out too. Why don't you sing, Dell?"

I've got a good voice. My freshman chorus teacher said I have "perfect pitch." He wanted me to try out for Vocal Ensemble, which is the honors chorus he runs. They always win first place in the state competition. They sing at all of our assemblies—and they even sang the national anthem at a Phillies game last year. They're freaking good. But they sing *in front* of people. I don't like an audience.

I sing to my little sister, Meggie. I sing in Cara's bedroom, but I make her turn the other way so she isn't looking at me. One time Cara cried when I sang *Angel* by Sarah McLachlan. She even showed me her goose bumps. She told me I have a gift, and she's been bugging me to perform in a talent show since seventh grade.

"Why don't I sing? Hmmm. Let's see. I'm picturing a moment of pure humiliation. Can you see it? Oh, I can see it." In an attempt to lighten the moment, I grab Cara's hand and pull it to my forehead. "There I am onstage, in that green dress I've wanted. The music starts, and it's so quiet that you can hear a pin drop. Or a *moo*. Can you hear the mooing? Listen, it's sort of low. But wait, there's a second cow in the audience. Oh yes, there it is. Wait . . . there's another one. I've missed my cue—the music is a few lines beyond where I was supposed to come in. I smile and bob my head so the audience thinks I know what I'm doing. Then you know what happens? I moo into the microphone. I bring the house down. The whole auditorium is hysterical. That, Cara Suddreth, is why I won't sing. In the talent show. In public. Ever. Any questions? Good. Period. End of story. Good night. The end."

Cara jerks her hand away and rolls her eyes. "You always think the worst, Dell. God. How do you know it would be like that? You don't *know* that."

"I know, that's all."

"You have a good voice. You should sing on a stage. Whatever."

"Whatever, back to you," I say. "Relax. Can't you take a joke?"

Again Cara rolls her eyes. "Me? Take a joke? I'm your best friend, Dell. All you ever do is joke."

Cleaning up My Anger

IT'S SATURDAY MORNING. MY EYES FLUTTER OPEN, and the first thought that pops into my head is: I hate how I look.

Like I said, I'm a big girl. You know the kind of fat when people say, "But she has such a pretty face"? Yeah, that's not me.

I'm fat and what you might call mannish-looking. That's what Taryn Anderson told me in sixth grade. She didn't even have the decency to say it *about* me. No, she said it right to my face.

My eyes are close together, and my brown hair is both

curly and frizzy, which is the worst hair possible. My nose is wide in the wrong place. My lips are the only thin part of me.

Mentally ripping myself to pieces is such a great way to start the day. I roll over and try to fall back asleep. It is pointless. I don't need an alarm clock on the weekend; I have my sister.

"Dehwy? I get out," Meggie says from her crib.

We've been in this cruddy apartment for over a year now. I don't mind sharing a room with my sister. I don't. But I miss my old room. It was double the size, with two big windows. This room is small, dark, and has the underlying odor of dirty diapers.

I stretch for a second and then get out of bed. "Good morning, Meggie-bideggie." I pick her and her pink-and-white checkered blanket up out of her crib (they're one unit), and I breathe my sister in. No matter how deeply I inhale, I can't hold on to her smell. My little sister smells pure and buttery and white and crisp and cinnamony and perfect. She smells like love. But I can never conjure her smell when I'm having a bad day. Like when I'm mooing or being excluded by Taryn's crowd.

I change Meggie's diaper and strap her into her high chair in record time. Meggie munches on Cheerios as I multitask, devouring a pile of frozen waffles and scrolling through my phone reading new texts from Cara. In between squishy/syrupy bites I text her back. She's been trying to get me to go to the mall today—which I can't do because I'm babysitting.

A drip of syrup falls on my phone screen. "Shit." I lick it off. Crisis averted.

"Shit," Meggie repeats.

I burst out laughing. "Meggie! Don't say that." I phony-scowl and shake my head.

She grins. "Shitshitshitshitshitshi—"

I reach over and cover her little mouth. She kisses my palm. I take my hand away and kiss her forehead. "Don't say that word. That's not a nice word. Okay?"

She grabs two handfuls of Cheerios and playfully shoves them in her mouth.

I take a big bite of waffle. "Chew, baby girl." If my mother wasn't at work, she'd reprimand both of us for not using our table manners. Then she'd give me crap for eating eight frozen waffles as one meal. She'd detail the following very important dietary points:

1. The box clearly says a serving size is two waffles. *Two*, Adele. Not eight.
2. Butter is pure fat. Why aren't you using that butter-flavored spray I bought you?

K. M. Walton

3. The regular syrup is for your sister and me. It's full
   of sugar. I bought you the sugar-free stuff, and you
   never use it.

I swipe the last bite of waffle around my plate to soak up
as much syrup as I can. I drag it through the puddle until
it's covered in brown gooey perfection. As I'm chewing, my
phone buzzes with a new text. Cara wants to go to the movies tonight. I might be able to go, depending on when my
mother gets off work. I text my mother to see when she'll be
home.

More buzzing. This time the text is from my father.

> I've proposed to Donna.
> We're heading to
> wine country for the week.
> Fly out this afternoon.
> Gotta cancel Sunday.
> I'll get you a T-shirt or
> something.

Proposed? To Donna? The sugary remnants of syrup rebel
in my mouth, and I gag. It's too sweet. I want to vomit. Panting and swallowing help to push the sick back down. I reread

the text. It is the official end of my family. My father isn't coming home. How could he propose to her and tell me in a text? This news is going to send my mother over the edge.

I read the text again, and the words "I proposed to Donna" cut me, through layers of skin and fat, and pierce my soul. My soul is screaming and bleeding and dying in there.

Dad and Donna instantly jump to numbers one and two on my "People I'd Like to Make Disappear" list.

I slam down my phone and punch the table so hard that the syrup bottle falls over and lands on its side. Meggie's lips quiver, and she bursts into tears.

I feel awful for scaring her. "Oh, baby girl. I'm sorry. Come here." I remove the tray from her high chair, unbuckle the strap, and lift Meggie and her blanket into a hug. "You're okay now." I kiss the top of her head, and Meggie sniffles.

My father has spent the last two years piling disappointment on disappointment. Cheating on my mother with Donna, leaving my mother before Meggie was born, refusing to keep up with his support payments, forcing us to sell our house and move away from my best friend, canceling so many "father-daughter weekends" that I can count the one that actually happened on a finger, and that was a total catastrophe.

I spent two days at my father's condo, holed up in the

guest room—which was about as inviting as a prison cell. It had a crappy single bed with scratchy sheets and a rock-hard pillow. There was a wooden chair in the corner with a lamp sitting on it, no dresser, no nightstand, no mirror. But it did have a small flat-screen TV—with cable—hanging on one wall.

I'd never watched more television in my life. When I was younger, my father was always turning off the cartoons and telling me to get outside and practice hitting. That weekend he wouldn't have noticed if I ate the TV. He spent both days "working," which I quickly realized was code for "spending the weekend with Donna."

Donna Ritch was (and still is) the ticket-taker at the parking garage that's attached to the building where my dad works. She's tall, skinny, young, and my baby sister is smarter than she is. Cara and I had lots of fun with her last name. Donna Bitch. Donna Witch. Donna Snitch. Donna Ditch.

When the rhyming got old, I named her Donna Dumbass. It works for me.

That father-daughter weekend, Dad had lunch with Donna Dumbass, had dinner with Donna Dumbass, and snuck Donna Dumbass home after dinner. They giggled and shushed each other up the stairs, while I was holed up in the prison-cell guest room. I cranked the volume on a riveting special about how killer whales communicate. It was better than the alternative.

Basically, the man has imploded his role as my father.

Or exploded.

However I look at it, my relationship with my father is broken—and now he's getting remarried. There won't be room for me in his new life. Not even a millimeter. Not that he's made room for me since he left. The only thing he's done for me over the past two years is pay for my phone. He pays for my mother's cell too. To be honest, I think he just forgot to have us kicked off his plan. I definitely wouldn't have my phone if my mother had to pay for it. She couldn't afford it.

I was supposed to spend the day with Dad at his condo tomorrow so we could work on my earth science project together. It was my idea. I actually opted not to have a partner so that I could work with my dad. I had cooked up a whole dreamy scenario in my head too. After helping me with my project, my father would realize how much he misses me—misses his old life—and he would come rescue us from our dumpy apartment like a knight in shining armor. Everything would go back to the way it used to be. My mother wouldn't need her pills. I wouldn't need my mounds of food. We'd be a family again.

I turn and growl at the brown paper bag filled with project supplies. The white Styrofoam balls and colorful wires peek out and taunt me.

I plop Meggie in front of her favorite TV show. With a purpose in my step, I head back into the kitchen. I wanted the bag and its contents to be more than they could. I wanted them to help me end the nightmare. The bag full of stuff should've given me a moment with my father. My old father. My pre-Donna, pre-selfish father.

I hate that bag and every single thing in it.

Before I can think, my foot launches the bag into the air, sending the contents flying all over the kitchen. Two plastic bottles crack as they land, and the kitchen is splattered with bright yellow and dark gray paint. A foam ball lands in my plate of leftover syrup; another rolls into the living room. The wires skitter across the floor, and that is that.

I pound on the counter a few times and let out a pretty decent yell. Meggie waddles in from the living room, dragging her blanket in one hand and holding the Styrofoam ball that had the good sense to run from my rage, in the other.

"What this?" Meggie asks, holding it up.

Breathless, I look down at her. "Nothing, Megs." She drops the ball and scurries back to her show. I survey the mess I created. That's when the tears come. I cry for everything

I've lost. I cry for the bright yellow paint, no longer happy or sunny, now that it's smeared over the grimy linoleum floor and dingy walls. I cry for the syrup-soaked Styrofoam ball, which is ruined. I cry because my father is never coming home.

I cry for it all.

Then I spend the next hour cleaning up my anger.

The World Whizzes By

AFTER I PUT MEGGIE DOWN FOR HER NAP, I MAKE myself a bowl of cereal. I use the large metal mixing bowl so I can load the sucker to the top. Each spoonful fills my mouth with sweet crunch and cold milk. I shut my eyes and concentrate on the brittle chomping sound my chewing makes. Every time my teeth clamp down, my heart unclenches a little inside my chest. My tongue moves everything where it needs to go, and I swallow and lick my lips. Over and over again.

My rage slowly fades. The spoon continues on its magical path from bowl to mouth. I'm halfway done, lost in my chewing and swallowing, when it registers: I'm full.

I look down into the bowl. There's still a fair amount of cereal left. This is the moment that I hate—when I ignore every signal, receptor message, or what-the-hell-ever it is that tells me I'm done. That my stomach is stuffed with food.

I pause and stare at the floating cereal. Like a witch stirs her cauldron, I swirl everything around with my spoon and mutter obscenities under my breath.

In midchurn I notice the drip of yellow paint on the table. It's the size of a crumb. My hand shakes as I reach over and try to rub it off with my finger. It doesn't budge. It's dry now. My fingernail slowly scratches back and forth over the dot of paint while my other hand feeds me the rest of the cereal. I open my mouth and let in every bite until the bowl is empty.

I wash out my bowl and put it away. My mother caught me eating cereal from it once before, and let's just say it was ugly. As I'm giving the kitchen a final once-over, looking for rogue paint splatters or any other evidence of my meltdown, I can't comprehend my father actually wanting to marry Donna Dumbass. I pace around the kitchen. How is my mother going to react to this new development? I know it will gouge another hole in her heart.

I realize that I want to piss off my father.

I text him back one word, "Whatever." He doesn't reply. Typical. He's morphed into a do-horrible-shit-and-then-act-like-I-didn't kind of guy. Don't get me wrong, he's not a loser. He is a genius—an aeronautical engineer, which means he designs airplanes. It's a cool job, but he's not cool. He thinks he is and wears black-frame glasses and Vans sneakers and expensive jeans. But he also cheated on his wife of fifteen years. He owes my mom a shitload in back child support, and he's making her go to court to get it, which is a total dick move. Last year he didn't call me on my birthday or get me a present because he was in Bermuda with "her." Birthdays were always his thing, too. Decorations, handmade signs, special breakfast place settings. Now there's none of that. He doesn't even remember my birthday anymore.

He doesn't know anything about Meggie, either. I think he's only seen her twice since she was born. She cried her eyes out the last time he tried to pick her up, and I had to step in to calm her down.

My phone buzzes.

> You should be happy for me.
> Stop beating me up please
> and just be happy for me.

He's a piece of work, that man.

I can feel my face getting hot again. What he fails to

recognize is how *un*happy the rest of us are. It's like his brain was removed from his skull, dipped in some kind of memory-erasing solution and replanted in his head. And he skipped happily along with Donna Dumbass, leaving my mother and me behind holding crumpled tissues filled with tears and snot and pain.

I go to put the cereal away, but I've eaten it all. The whole damn box. I give it another shake to be sure, and try to remember if it was a new box. I cringe. I had struggled to rip open the stupid plastic bag just ten minutes ago.

Our old fireplace would come in handy right now. I'd love to watch the box burn, the plastic bag melt, and the evidence of my binge get reduced to dust. Instead, I stamp on the box and fold it into the tiniest square possible, pushing it deep into the bottom of the trash can.

Something else I push down—trying to understand my father's actions. I gave up about a month after he left, and I started eating. Turns out food actually does have some magical powers because I feel full, like, un-hollow, after I eat. When I can't take one more bite, that is when I experience joy. Then I open my mouth again, and I want to punch myself in the face.

My mother's phone call cheers me up. She tells me that I can go to the movies with Cara. This is exactly what I needed to hear. I keep my father's proposal to myself. I don't want to

K. M. Walton

bum my mother out; she sounded happy because she's getting out of work early.

Work for my mother now involves two jobs—one at the pharmacy in town and a weekend job at FoodMart. After my father left, my mom couldn't be a stay-at-home mom anymore. We had to sell our four-bedroom, two-and-a-half-bath house with the big backyard because Dad refused to keep up the payments and Mom couldn't afford it on her own. We've already blown through our share of the money they got for selling the house with living expenses. Turns out my mom's portion—twenty-one thousand—goes pretty quickly with two kids, one of whom is in diapers.

Our two-bedroom apartment is in a multibuilding complex off a major road. It has stained carpets, a permanent ring around the toilet, and you can hear the traffic all day and night. Just outside the door to our building, there's this tiny patch of grass that's usually filled with cigarette butts and chewed gum—that's our yard.

This is my mother's new life.

This and her pills. Mom now takes pills to wake up in the morning. She takes pills to help her sleep at night. She takes pills to calm her nerves and pills for her depression. She takes pills to lower her blood pressure and stop her heartburn and deal with her allergies. I think the pharmacy hired my mother because she's their best customer. She knows her drugs. The pharmacist always jokes that my mom should be filling the prescriptions instead of ringing people up at the register.

I give Meggie a bath, feed her dinner, and am tucking her into bed just as my mother gets in from work. She stands in the doorway, looking wiped out. There are dark circles under her eyes and some sort of blue stain down the front of her yellow FoodMart shirt.

"How's my Megs?" She smiles at my sister. She turns to me and, in a completely different tone, says, "Don't you have a better top to wear?" She yawns.

Sometimes I hate my mother. I do. She doesn't understand my body and how nothing but the crap I wear makes me look presentable. I've learned to stop arguing with her. It makes our time together less explosive.

A horn honks out front.

"Cara's here," I say.

Mom stares, obviously waiting for me to address her wardrobe comment.

"Mother, don't you think I would wear something else if it fit me?" I leave the aggravation out of my tone. I don't want an argument to erupt while Cara's waiting.

"Your grandmother bought you extra large. For God's sake, those clothes have to fit you."

K. M. Walton

Why does she refuse to listen to me?

"I don't know, Mom." I have nothing else to say on the matter. Cara's honks again. "I like—"

She interrupts. "Don't tell me you like those T-shirts. I can't hear it again. I don't know either, Adele. I don't know anything anymore."

We look at each other silently. I wonder if my own mother sees me. As with Cara, I don't think she does. Mom's eyes are clouded over with exhaustion and whatever concoction of pills she's on at the moment.

Sadness releases from my chest. Like a snake, it slithers down my legs. I swear I feel its mouth bite into my thigh. Its miserable venom seeps into my bloodstream. I grind my teeth together to stop the sadness from penetrating my brain, my heart . . . my soul.

"Just go, before she honks again and that nut Mr. Xien calls the police."

I walk down the hallway with clenched fists. The anger swirls together with the sadness, creating a perfect storm of awful. After I close the door behind me, I jump up and down a few times on the landing to shake off the unhappiness.

"What did your parents say about you getting cut?" Cara asks as we pull out.

"Nothing."

"Nothing?" Her face contorts into a scowl. Apparently my answer annoys her.

I shrug.

"You didn't tell them, did you?"

I don't really care what either of my parents thinks right now.

"Don't you think they'll notice, Dell?"

"Don't care."

"Huh."

We get quiet because that's what we do in these situations. These moments are uncomfortable. Sometimes I create this fantasy that our silence is rich with understanding and support. So stupid.

I want Cara to be proud of me for not caring what my parents think and tell me that softball doesn't matter because we've got each other. Maybe she could even look over and smile at me when she says it.

From the corner of my eye, I watch her turn on the radio and tap the steering wheel. I grip the edge of the front seat. She bobs her head to the beat. "I think everyone's going to be there tonight, Dell."

By "everyone," I suspect she means Taryn's and Brandon's crew. But there has never been an "everyone" before. It's usually just the two of us. "At the movies?"

She huffs. "Yeah, Dell, at the movies."

This is the second time she's gotten annoyed with me in less than two minutes. It's some kind of craptastic record. My fingertips press deeper into the seat cushion, and I feel the cloth give a little. I let go. Poking a hole in Cara's mother's front seat would definitely infuriate her. I don't want Cara to be mad at me. I need her.

As we drive in silence the world outside whizzes by in a blur. Inside the car I'm doing my best to act like everything's normal. I abandon my death grip on the upholstery and tap my thigh to the music. Despite my lighthearted outward appearance, horrible thoughts take up all of the space in my brain. The most awful? My friendship with Cara just isn't the same anymore. It doesn't feel right. Or comfortable.

We sit at the light, waiting to make the left, and I want to tell Cara to turn around and take me home. "Oh, it's so packed!" Cara exclaims. I can hear the excitement in her voice. The movie theater parking lot *is* a madhouse. People are everywhere, and Cara slows down to a crawl. "Sydney's gotta be here," Cara whispers to herself.

We drive up and down the rows, looking for a spot. Cara jams her foot on the brake, and we come to a screeching halt as three girls with matching cheerleading jackets, identical ponytails, and ribbons suddenly appear in front of our car. "God! Watch where you're—" Cara cuts herself off, sticks her head out the open window, and purrs in the most over-the-top chipper voice, "Girls, you look so cuu-uute."

The girls pause. They turn in unison, giving Cara smiles as sugary as her compliment. The one in the middle with the black hair and perfect face says, "Grassy-ass, bay-bee." She blows Cara a kiss and then folds in half, laughing herself to pieces. Cara starts clapping and giggling. My eyebrows are sewn together in what-the-hell-is-going-on-here confusion.

The black-haired beauty straightens herself and holds out her arms. Her friends, as if by magnetic force, link arms with her. They skip through the parking lot like they're in a field of wildflowers.

"Holy crap, Dell, that was Brandon Levitt's little sister. The pretty one in the middle. Maybe she'll put in a good word for us."

I can't look at Cara because my face will show how I feel inside—nauseated. I keep my gaze straight ahead. "Wow."

We end up having to park really far away from the movie theater. "Bring the map in case we get lost," I joke. I'm trying to snap myself out of how disgusted I feel after watching that phony interaction. Cara doesn't respond to my attempt at humor. She's busy studying her face and puckering her lips in the visor mirror. Then she walks the entire way to the theater door on her tippie toes, scanning the rows of cars, obviously

K. M. Walton

looking for "everyone." Remarkably, the only people we see from school are the other freshman cheerleaders. They seriously all have matching ponytails and ribbons. Yeah. I mean, my softball team used to wear our team T-shirts to school on game days, but I've never gone out in public, just for fun, dressed the same as someone else.

Standing in the line for food, I stare at the illuminated menu. If I had thirty dollars in my pocket, I could easily spend it: large popcorn, large soda, two boxes of candy, and a hot dog. I only have a ten, though. Small popcorn, a box of candy, no drink. I douse my popcorn in butter. It's so much better with the butter.

I follow Cara like a puppy dog through the hallway, lost in my own thoughts. Maybe I'll get a job now that softball doesn't have a chokehold on my time. Then I could buy whatever the hell I wanted at the movies. I could even save for a car. I'd drive and drive and drive—to get away.

Cara stops suddenly just inside our theater, and I bump into her. "Dell, God, watch where you're going! You made me spill my soda."

"Sorry." I hand her the wad of napkins I'd grabbed for eating my popcorn, and she wipes off her jeans.

For how crazy the parking lot and lobby were, our theater is pretty empty, only a few older couples and those cheerleaders in the back row, and that's it. "Everyone" must be seeing something else.

Cara squints and mumbles, "Where is everyone?" I follow her up a few stairs and we take our seats. Cara offers me one of her soft-pretzel bites.

I take one and dip it in the warm cheese sauce. As the spicy cheese has its way with my tongue, I wonder why food that isn't good for you tastes so damn delicious. Green beans or cheese sauce? Cheese sauce, please. I'd eat the green beans *with* the cheese sauce. No doubt.

Those girls in the back row are being obnoxious, laughing too loud, squealing, shouting. "I hope they don't do that during the movie," I say.

Cara drops her feet from their perch on the seatback in front of her and turns completely around.

"Oh my God, Cara, don't say anything," I whisper and shrink down a bit.

Cara's face lights up, and she starts waving. "Hold this. I'll be right back." She hands me her pretzel-bite tray, scurries across the aisle, and disappears up the steps. I can't believe she went to say hi to them.

Her pretzels gaze up at me, each piece of salt a sympathetic eye—staring, feeling deeply sorry for me. I think these pretzels understand me more than Cara ever has.

A few minutes pass. *Has Cara abandoned me?* Her laugh reaches their volume, and I slide farther down in my seat. The advertisement for Rocco's Italian Palace taunts me from the screen. The mounds of lasagna and garlic bread, displayed on a red-and-white checkered tablecloth, look so good I can almost taste the garlic. I eat one of Cara's pretzels instead and listen to the girls' voices. Despite how loud they are back there, I can't make out much of what they are saying. I'm midchew when one word slices through the noise: *fat.* My whole body freezes and I hyper-focus. More uproarious laughter, and then there it is again: *fat.* My stomach drops, and I cringe as I swallow the dough and salt.

Now the salt-eyes can see me from the inside. The private me. The real me. Will they still be sympathetic?

I drop my chin and stare into my boobs. I am a freak. One of the older women in the back tries to shush them. A girl shouts, "It's a free country, lay-dee!" I'm pretty sure that was Brandon's little sister.

Cara returns, skipping across our row of seats toward me. *Shit, she's a skipper now.* I look down at Cara's tray. "Great," I announce. I've eaten all but two of her pretzel bites. She notices as soon as she sits down.

"Geez, Dell. I asked you to hold them, not eat them."

I hold out my popcorn.

"No. I don't want that. Whatever." She checks her phone

and then shoves it back into her pocket. "You saved me the calories anyway."

I'm waiting for her to tell me why she went up there, to tell me what they said. Maybe even apologize for not inviting me up and introducing me.

She doesn't.

"I applied for a summer internship at West Chester University last night. My dad helped me with my essay." Cara shoves a drippy pretzel bite into her mouth, leans over, and whispers, "He wro tha whole thin." She swallows. "He wrote the whole thing," she clarifies. I eat a handful of butter-soaked popcorn.

The last pretzel bite finds its way to her mouth. She nods and says, "He's awesome."

"Nice." My father wouldn't write an essay *with* me, let alone *for* me. I crunch on more popcorn.

"I wonder where everyone is. Sydney said they were seeing this movie too."

The theater goes dark, so I don't have to hide my disappointment. Right now would be the ideal time for some magical intervention—presto, I'm gone.

Cara is slipping away from me. I'm starting to feel like I'm a nuisance, Cara's annoying fat friend who just won't shrivel up and go away. Instead, I get bigger and bigger.

I lick the greasy butter from each finger and crumple the

popcorn bag. I'm still hungry. Small portions are unsatisfy-ingly frustrating. Like when I was a kid in the sandbox, and I'd packed the bucket with dry sand, pushing it down real tight, then turned it over, expecting to see a sand castle, but it col-lapsed into nothing. I used to hate when that happened.

As gunfire explodes on-screen, my phone buzzes in my pocket. I jump a little. It's a text from my father. He has used all caps. He's pissed. I excuse myself and tell Cara I have to go to the bathroom. I refuse to read the text until I'm in the pri-vacy of a stall. Whatever he has texted will infuriate me.

Apparently the people who design bathrooms are skinny, because I can barely maneuver my body inside to close the door. No one else is around, which is good, and I slam the door and the entire row of stalls shakes. I don't actually have to go to the bathroom, so I stand in the stall. It is a damn tight squeeze. I feel like the wicked stepsister's foot crammed into the glass slipper. I'm already breathing heavily, mostly out of frustration. "God!" I yell.

I read the stupid text from my stupid father:

> I CAN'T UNDERSTAND WHY YOU
> REFUSE TO BE HAPPY FOR ME
> AFTER ALL I'VE DONE FOR YOU.
> CALL ME!

Yeah.

I wipe hot tears from my cheeks and sniffle. How can I be happy for him when he announced that he was getting remarried in a text message? He didn't consider me or how I'd feel. Other than hating her, I don't know Donna—and now she's going to be married to my father. My family will never be whole again. We will be broken forever.

I make this choking/coughing sound as I sob into my bent elbow.

I don't want to call him. In fact, I'd prefer he and DD sneak off to go live in their fairy-tale land instead of shoving his happiness down my throat. Maybe the wicked stepmother could put a curse on them. Or a dragon could eat them both.

I grab a handful of toilet paper and blow my nose. I can feel the sweat on the back of my neck. I have to get out of this sausage stall. I walk straight outside to the sidewalk because I'm suffocating. Once I catch my breath I text him back:

I quit softball.

After I hit send, my heart races. That is going to piss him off more than my "Whatever." I want my lie to make him go nuts. It would be satisfying to hear the way Dad's voice slides down an octave when he's furious. I want to hurt him as much

K. M. Walton

as he has hurt me. Maybe I'm a glutton for punishment, but I want to talk to him. Maybe it'll make me feel alive. I dial his number. After a few rings, he picks up.

Dad shouts, "What do you mean *you quit*?"

"I mean, I quit."

Heavy, exasperated breathing fills my ear.

I whisper, "You're marrying her?"

"This isn't a good time. Donna and I are about to get massages."

I swear to God he says this.

Now it's my turn to huff in *his* ear.

"Adele, I don't know why that coach didn't cut you last season. You aren't in shape. Congratulations on blowing any chance you had for a college scholarship."

I repeat my one-word eff-you, "Whatever." Him exploding right now would be the perfect vindication.

"I'm allowed to be happy!" he yells. "Do you hear me? I'm allowed to be happy, damnit!"

I say nothing. Dad's anger isn't having the desired effect. I feel limp and tired, and just want to plop in bed and disappear underneath the covers.

I shiver as misery seeps from my pores. I press the phone to my ear, but I don't say anything. Couples and families stream by me. I watch a father and his two young daughters. The guy's got one girl on either side of him, and he's holding their hands, laughing and smiling. He looks down at his children with the best expression. Love.

I want someone to look at me like that. Accept me, love me, see me.

"Don't you answer me with one word. Do you—" There's rustling and then Donna Dumbass says something, but I can't make out the words. Dad says to her, "I'm fine, honey. I'm fine. She's just, ah, being difficult."

DD must lean in, on purpose, because I hear her clearly say to my father, "*I* love you."

"I love you more."

If there was any kind of sharp, pointy object within reach, it would be firmly implanted in my eye.

"Listen to me, Adele," my father starts back at me. "Donna makes me happy. I love her, and you're going to have to learn to love her too."

I swallow a scream and cough loudly in his ear. On purpose.

My father clears his throat. "Just because you are overweight and angry about it, that's no reason for you to lash out at me. I did not make you overweight."

My stomach feels like it met the fist of a prizefighter.

"My mother even bought you all of those nice clothes." I

K. M. Walton

hear him say to Donna, "She's holding everything against me, even her weight."

I wipe away a tear and whisper, "Me being fat is none of your business. I was fine before you ruined everything. You act like I don't exist."

"I did not call you fat, Adele. Were you even listening to me? I think me finding happiness may have something to do with your overeating," he says.

"I . . . have to . . . go," I choke out.

"Don't blame me for—"

I hang up on him. On my way back to the bathroom to splash water on my face, I pray that the massage therapist uses boiling-hot oil. I want their tender, exposed skin to feel pain. Pure, raw pain. Because that is what I feel.

I eventually go back to the theater. As I slide into my seat, Cara whispers, "Jeez, Dell, did you fall in?"

"Ha-ha," I say, and nothing more.

The Obvious Conclusion

AFTER THE MOVIE ENDS, CARA AND I BLEND IN WITH the crowd exiting from other movies and stream outside. Off to the left is a huge group of kids from school congregating on the sidewalk. Cara yanks me to a stop and commands, "Hold on." I lean with my back against the building and try to look casual.

Cara is up on her toes again. "Do you see Sydney in there? I can't see her." She rummages through her purse for something. She pulls out her phone and talks to me as she texts. "I think we could, you know, break in with Sydney. She's been talking to me in French class, Dell." She looks up at me. "I just told her that we're here."

"Cara!" a voice squeals. Sydney materializes in front of us. Her hair is so pretty. It's honey blond, straight, and shiny, and *I* want to pet it. I look her up and down. Cute jeans, tight V-neck tee with just a bit of her stomach showing. Sydney flashes a huge smile. "Hey, what did you guys see? She looks directly at Cara. I don't even get a glance.

Cara bounces as she talks. "The one with the soldiers and stuff." She turns to me. "What was the name of it, Dell?"

I shrug. I have no idea. I missed half of it, and the parts I saw were a blur.

Sydney says, "Oh my God, Cara, we saw *Robot Nation*. So stupid. The whole theater was packed. Some idiots from school were throwing popcorn and shouting, but the guy in the movie had the hottest abs."

"Kyle Wolf?" Cara yelps. "He *is* gorgeous! I love him."

Kyle Wolf? Who the hell is Kyle Wolf? How does my best friend love a gorgeous actor and his abs, yet I've never heard of him?

Sydney and Cara ping-pong back and forth about Kyle's other hot body parts. I pull out my phone and pretend I'm busy texting someone. I wonder why Sydney didn't tell Cara that everyone was seeing *Robot Nation*. My eyes focus on my pudgy fingers, and I wonder no more. Cara wasn't told because those girls don't want to be seen with me.

"Dell!" I hear from deep in the crowd.

I turn. It's Brandon. He saddles up beside me. He reeks of alcohol.

"Yo! Dell! Sup?" he shouts.

"Nothing," I say. God, he looks hot. With his smile and those long, dark eyelashes.

He turns around and shouts, "Chase! Cah-mere! Look, it's Dell!"

Chase pushes through the other kids, dragging two other guys with him. Their eyes all have that glazed look. They're shit-faced.

Chase raises his hand to high-five me and slurs, "Yo! Doooo it!" He turns to Brandon and leans on him. "Maker do it, B-man."

Brandon's face lights up and there's nodding and he gives me that enormous smile. "Come on, Dell. It so funny." He puts his tongue between his lips and blows a loud raspberry, clearly amused with his verbal mistake. "I mean, *it's* so funny. You're so funny, Dell." All of a sudden Brandon's head is on my shoulder and he's rubbing my arm. "Please."

My cheeks get hot. Brandon's hand is warm on my skin. My whole body has a heat surge—blood is on the move, flowing and coursing—sending prickles up my spine. He thinks I'm funny. And he has his head on my shoulder. I can smell his spicy shampoo.

K. M. Walton

"Pleeeeease," he begs. My nostrils are assaulted by his alcohol breath. The arm-stroking stops, and he looks me in the eye. I try to decipher if drunk-Brandon can really see me. I wonder if alcohol has the ability to make one human being see another human being. I search for any sign of this. In two seconds I realize that I can't even lock on to his eyes because they're rolling around in their sockets.

Cara stops her riveting conversation with Sydney about who would pay more money to see Kyle Wolf naked, grabs my forearm, and giggles. "Just do it, Dell. They're so wasted."

"Yeah. Wasted and hot," Sydney chimes in.

I look over at Brandon. He's now holding on to Chase for dear life as they drunk-teeter back and forth. They each have the biggest, stupidest grins on their faces. My face slides into a smile. I've liked Brandon since seventh grade, and that's a long time. I think I fell for him when he complimented the grand slam I hit during gym. He said, because I remember it verbatim, "Hey, Dell, killer hit. You have a good swing." He said it in the nicest voice. I remember my stomach had flip-flopped, and I'd bumbled out a thank-you. Then he smiled and bit his lip, and I blushed.

Since then, I've fantasized about him asking me out. He only dates the most popular girls—beautiful girls. I am not, nor will I ever be, beautiful. Even if I were thin. I think he views me as one of the guys. Just another fellow athlete, not a girl.

Now, there's this whole mooing thing. It's my fault that he keeps begging me to do it. I started it. I did it in gym last year to be funny. I made fun of myself before anyone else could. What I do has a name: self-deprecation. I saw it on TV. I don't really care what it's called. It worked. I just never expected that I'd still be mooing for others' entertainment.

Brandon whines, "Come on, Dell. Do it."

I look to Cara and desperately want her to shake her head, mouthing, "No." It would be so cool if she would tell them all to go to hell, but she's not even paying attention anymore. She and Sydney are busy putting on lip gloss.

Cara freezes with her hand in midair, lip gloss wand clutched between her fingers. "What's the big deal? Just do it. Everyone's waiting."

So I sumo-pose, I moo, and I bring the sidewalk down. Chase practically falls over. Cara and Sydney laugh so hard they dab the corners of their eyes. A few other guys imitate my moo and high-five each other.

Once he catches his breath, Brandon turns to Sydney and Cara. "We're going to Melissa's house. You guys wanna come?"

Before they even have a second to respond, I open my mouth. "Yeah. I'm in."

K. M. Walton

After he walks away, Cara looks at me with eyebrows raised. "Oh my God." Her smile tells me she's excited. We've never been invited to one of these parties. *My* smile fades as we head to Cara's car because I'm not sure if she was shocked that she got invited or because I invited myself. We're about to make quite the party team: Beauty and the Beast.

I get my answer when she asks me if I'll drive. "Okay, sure." She tosses me the keys and begins a full-on texting bonanza with Sydney. In the ten minutes it takes to get to Melissa's house, I'm privy to a whole lot of mumbling as Cara reads text after text after text. Something about a song they both love, and how hot Sydney thinks Chase is, and what she plans to drink at the party. There are even a few reactionary bursts of laughter from Cara. I'm not in on the joke. My eyes stay focused on the road ahead, and I don't bother questioning her about anything.

I just drive.

A Solid Block of Ice

MELISSA'S HOUSE IS FILLED WITH THIRTY OR FORTY juniors. Most of the girls are drinking wine coolers, and the guys all have beer. Smoke wafts up from the basement each time someone opens or closes the door. I think most of the kids were drunk or high before the party started.

From my vantage point on the sofa, I witness some wild stuff. Two girls are making out, surrounded by a circle of guys. Chase and Sydney are going at it on Melissa's dad's recliner, and it looks as if Sydney's going to be topless for the world to see any second. While we were standing on the sidewalk at the movie theater, she'd pulled her hair up into one of those sloppy ponytails. Well, it's beyond sloppy now. Half of her hair has escaped the rubber band, and she doesn't even notice. She's too busy slurping Chase's face off and grinding his crotch.

Melissa, Emma, and Cara are in another corner, jumping around to the blaring music. They repeatedly smash into one another. Melissa keeps falling down, and Emma keeps picking her back up again.

Cara's been jumping ever since we walked in. I don't want to be mad at her. I want her to have fun. Getting invited to one of these parties has sort of been her dream since the end of sophomore year. She's definitely having fun—I can tell by the size of her smile. She's blissfully lost in the jumping. I'm lost here in the sofa cushions.

I know I could make the effort and join them, but if I jumped, there'd be a strong chance I'd bust through the hard-wood floor and land in the basement in a heap of splintered wood and concrete. The stoners would have the laugh of the century. The party would be ruined.

Cara fits in perfectly with those girls. They all like jump-ing around. They all fling their hair the same way. They all dress in cute clothes. They're all skinny and pretty.

Cara skips over and stands in front of me, breathless. "C-ome on, Dell. It's so fun!"

"Nah, I'm good." I give her an enthusiastic thumbs-up. I'm

kind of shocked she even broke contact with them to invite me over. A twinge of relief, or maybe it's happiness, comes to life in my heart. Cara didn't forget me. My mouth slides into a half grin.

"Okay." She wipes the sweat from her forehead and says, "You're smiling, so you must be all right over here." Cara rejoins the jumpers. I finish my beer and silently wish she'd begged me to join them. Her "okay" came way too easy. If it were reversed, I would've put a little more oomph into my plea. But that's just me.

I'm on my fourth beer when I start thinking about my effed-up parents. The conversation with my father and my mother's admission that she doesn't "know anything anymore" play on a loop. I'm a regular ball of party-animal fun.

I'm about to get up and grab another beer when Brandon emerges from the basement in a cloud of smoke. He gives me a very slow nod and saunters over. Plopping down next to me, his head continues bobbing, like a toy. "It's a weed fest down there."

I scan the room. "Where's Taryn?" His girlfriend is typically glued to his side.

"Not here. Had some shit to do with her family. Don't care."

"Huh," I say. I want to tell him that he looks hot and that I like the way his black hair curls out from under his baseball hat and how his faded T-shirt with the old-fashioned Phillies logo hugs his chest and arms perfectly. But I don't. I haven't had that many beers.

"Wannaseesomething?" Brandon slurs. His blue eyes are glassy and tinged with red. He leans in and whispers in my ear, "Do you?"

I know how the world works. Life is not a fairy tale. I know I am double Brandon's weight. I know he has the hottest girlfriend on the planet. I know he's the baseball team's star pitcher. I know he's insanely popular. I get all of this. So how come I can picture him kissing me here on this couch?

"You wanna see something?" he repeats in my ear. The scent of his shampoo fills my nose again. I close my eyes and inhale.

It's hard to concentrate, but I am curious. "Depends on what it is."

"Come on, you'll think it's hill-freakin'-larious." He stands, sways a little, and puts out his hand to help me up. How gentlemanly. I know better than to accept it. I do not need a trashed Brandon Levitt struggling to help me stand up. No way.

"I'm good. I got it," I shout over the music. Thankfully he turns and misses my ballerina-like grace as I try to heave myself out of the sofa. At first I can't do it because the cushion is suction-cupped around me. Plus, I'm kind of tipsy. I rock back and grunt. No go. I repeat the rocking motion and finally pull my ass out of the sofa-hole. Perched on the edge of the couch, I'm out of breath.

Brandon's waiting for me at the foot of the stairs, and I want to hide. He had to have seen my pathetic attempt at getting up. I still need a beer. I take a deep breath and push up hard to get myself to standing. An involuntary groan escapes, and I squeeze my hands into fists. I know he's watching me.

We make eye contact, and Brandon smiles, so I guess that's good. I point to my beer, he nods, and I head into the kitchen to grab a fresh can from the fridge.

Four girls from softball are playing flip cup with four guys from the baseball team. They've pulled the kitchen table into the center of the room. The table and floor are soaked in beer. I grab a new beer from the fridge, unnoticed. I crack it open and take a long drink.

This kitchen is huge and shiny. Everything looks new. The white tile floor, the marble countertops, the stainless steel appliances—all glisten and sparkle, reminding me that my kitchen is depressing.

One of the girls squeals so loudly that I startle in midsip, and beer dribbles down my chin and onto my chest. "Great,"

I mumble to myself. I cringe on my way out, because the eight of them around that table couldn't possibly be any louder.

"Hey, we need a judge!" one of the guys shouts. I turn around and stare at them. The boys all have the same buzz haircut. How cute. Two other dudes have come into the kitchen and are making their way to the fridge. I assume he's talking to one of them.

"Yo, we're talking to you!" the same guy barks, and he points at me this time. I think his name is Jacob.

Oh.

"Come on, Dell, judge for us!" Amy, my former softball teammate, pleads.

I peek into the living room. Brandon is gone. I wouldn't have waited for me either. I walk toward the table. "Okay."

Apparently the guys think the girls are cheating somehow, so they feel they need a referee. I get the rules from Amy, and presto, I am the official judge of this flip-cup game. The girl side of the table crushes the boys with four straight wins. I celebrate each win with a long chug of beer. After the fifth fair-and-square manhandling by the girls, the guys are getting agitated. Jacob drunkenly argues every call I make, punches the table, and shoves the guy next to him. Now I know why he wanted a judge—he couldn't believe the girls were legitimately killing it. Truthfully, I don't know how anyone is winning. We're all drunk.

Jacob squints at me and runs his hand over the brown fuzz on his head. "Why are you making that face?" he shouts. "What's your problem?"

I'm making a face? Wow, someone took their aggressive pills. Before I can answer him, Amy slurs, "Leave her alone, Jacob. She got cut from softball 'cause she's toofattoplay." All four girls' eyes bulge. They crumble into laughter, grasping the sides of the table, and then slump into piles on the wet floor. It is quite the moment of hilarity.

Normally I'd laugh right along with them to let them know that they didn't hurt me with their words. But what I'd like to do is grab them by the backs of their necks and smash their faces into the table. One by one.

Tonight, right now, I give them zero reaction. I don't even blink.

"Ooooh, scary death stare," Jacob taunts.

I'm working hard to muster my most maniacal serial-killer look, and it's giving me an inner adrenaline surge. Each pump of my heart pulses liquid power through my veins. If I closed my eyes and concentrated, I bet I could fly right now. Instead, I focus on staying stone-faced and staring.

Jacob puffs out his cheeks in a "fat person" imitation. So

K. M. Walton

original. I roll my eyes. In a flash he reaches underneath the table and lifts his side up in the air. The red plastic cups slide off and bounce around the kitchen. "Hold on, everyone, she's tilting the whole fucking planet!" Jacob yells. Empty beer cans rattle to the floor. One was apparently full, because when it lands, white foam shoots from it like a geyser. The four girls squeak and yelp and burst into giggles. I stare at the amber waterfall running off the table. It sounds like a gushing river as it hits the tiles—soothing in a way.

The fact that the word "soothing" just came to mind after my being degraded like that is funny. My mouth slides into a smile, and I rupture into uncontrolled laughter. I don't want to laugh; I want to glare at Jacob with laser-beam eyes, but I've lost it. It must be the beer. I. Am. Drunk.

"Someone pop her. S-someone pah—" He can't finish because he's laughing his ass off. The table slips from his grip and slams to the floor. Two of the girls roll around in a tangled heap of howling. One guy has his hands on his knees, crying-laughing. It's a goddamn riot in here.

Where is Cara? My best friend—my only friend. I want to laugh with her. I wipe away my tears and sweat and try to compose myself. Why am I laughing? The flashy white-ness of the room smears when I blink, and I swear the ground wobbles. I reach for something to hold on to. There's nothing there, and I stumble. The center island stops my momentum. I lay my head down on the cold marble and breathe.

I want another beer.

The chilly blast from the fridge feels awesome on my face. I grab a drink for me, one for Brandon. The cans are freezing in my hands. I grip them tightly and silently beg the cold to travel up my arms and settle in my heart. I'd like my heart to be a solid block of ice. Impenetrable. I am in a room full of assholes. I want to get out.

Cara and the jumping girls are gone when I reach the living room. *Where did everyone go?* I have to go to the bathroom. I look down the hall and see the open door. There's no one in line. It's a miracle. I stagger in and barely get seated before peeing my pants. The tiny powder room begins to close in on me. I lean my head on the wall. Someone's knocking. "I'm in here!" I shout.

"Hurry up," a female voice replies.

That bitch is going to have to wait. I scrunch my nose. "Get Cara." *She can help me. Cara, I need you.* I'm crying now. Tears stream down my cheeks. When I go to lift my head, I can't. It feels permanently attached to the wall.

"What did you say?" More knocking. "Come on!"

The knocking startles me, and the wall-head connection is broken. I pull toilet paper from the roll and blow my nose.

Bang. Bang. Bang. "Are you puking in there or what?"

I don't respond. I sob into my hand.

Bang. Bang. Bang. "What the hell are you doing? Hurry up!"

I hoist myself up and watch everything swirl around in the bowl after I flush. I change my gaze and try to focus on my reflection in the mirror. Everything's blurry. *Why did I drink so many beers? Shit.* "Stop banging," I mumble. It's so annoying. I wipe my face, then fling open the door midbang.

I'm nose-to-nose with Emma, who's friends with Sydney and Melissa. "Move!" she commands. I take one step forward, an unopened beer in each hand. She squeezes by me and slams the door.

Amy is next in line. "You take forever," she states flatly. I nod and continue back to my sofa-hole.

The music is still pumping, and Chase and Sydney are still grinding on the recliner. I look around for Brandon. He's sitting on the steps again. He cups his mouth and shouts to Chase, "Get a room!"

Chase doesn't stop making out with Sydney, but he does give Brandon the finger.

When Brandon sees me, he stands up. His eyes are slits, and he's got a perma-grin. I hand him a fresh beer and pop a piece of gum in my mouth. He watches me chew. "Hey, ki-hava-piece?"

Before I can reach into my pocket, he grabs my hand. "Gimme it up here," he says. His grip is firm and definite as he leads me up the stairs. I squeeze his hand—I want him to know how much I like his touch. In what feels like slow motion, he looks over his shoulder, grasps my hand tighter, and puckers his lips. I giggle. I am holding hands with Brandon Levitt, being led upstairs as he blows me air-kisses.

With each step up the stairs, the noise of the music fades. I like how quiet it is at the top.

Alone with the Daisies

"IN HERE." BRANDON STUMBLES INTO THE WALL and then pushes open the door to Melissa's parents' room. "It's on YouTube."

Melissa's mother is deeply in love with daisies. The whole room explodes with them. The walls, the bedspread, the pillows, the curtains, the fake flower arrangements. There are even framed pictures of daisies.

"Wow," I say. I sway a bit and reach out for the door frame.

He blinks slowly when he talks. "What?"

"Lots of flowers in here."

"Huh?"

I let it go.

"Over here." Brandon leads me to the desk with a computer. The seat cushion is daisy-fied. So is the notepad to the left of the keyboard. He gestures for me to take the chair, then he leans over me, clicking on stuff. His manly deodorant and the beer on his breath fill my nose. His forearm brushes my shoulder, his touch sending sparkly, glittery energy straight to my— I cut myself off. *What the hell? Sparkly, glittery energy? You really are drunk.* I bite the inside of my cheek.

He stands back and says, "Watch this."

I chew my gum and try to focus. It's a short video clip of a sumo wrestler. The wrestler falls over for no apparent reason, and then he can't get back up. He tries and tries, but he just can't do it. This is cracking Brandon up—he's hyperventilating behind me.

I smack my knee for effect. I am not even sure if people actually do this or if it just happens in the movies, but regardless, I smack mine and laugh hard for Brandon.

"I know, right? H . . . he . . ." Brandon can't get the words out. "When he rolls—ohmyGodohmyGod. When he rolls over." *He* smacks his knee. "His fat ass jiggles."

I run my hand along my sweating beer and use the water to swipe the back of my neck. I feel faint. I need to get out of this room. I stagger to the door. "So funny." I swallow my gum by mistake. The minty-fresh gob slides down my throat, and I gag. *Please don't puke in front of Brandon,* I plead in my mind.

He is in front of me like a flash, standing in the doorway with this puppy-dog smile. "Don't go, Dell." It's the same tone of voice he used to compliment my grand slam.

The gagging sensation subsides. I smile. I can feel my nothing-lips disappear up into my gums. I wish I had lips like Taryn's. Plump and sexy enough to make a guy want to kiss me.

"Don't go," he repeats.

He must want me to hold his beer while he pees, or maybe he has to puke and he needs me to stay with him.

"Fine. Yougottapee?" I ask in one long word.

He shakes his head.

I squeeze my eyebrows together. "What, then?"

Brandon leans in and says all breathy in my ear, "I want you . . . to stay."

His answer doesn't register in my beer-soaked brain. Brandon begs me to moo in front of people. He just showed me a video of a fat, diapered Japanese dude's ass, which I'm sure reminded him of me. There is no way Brandon Levitt is asking me to stay with him in this daisy bedroom. This bedroom with a ginormous bed.

No way.

He takes my hand without saying a word and leads me to

the bed. He puts his beer on the nightstand, takes my beer and places it next to his, and then sits me down. He stands directly in front of me and yanks off his baseball hat. With both hands he tousles his hair. I can't believe how hot he is. Then he pulls his T-shirt over his head and drops it on the floor.

I. I. I . . .

In a single motion, he yanks down his jeans and boxers and kicks them to the side. I have never seen a naked guy before. Well, I've seen them from the waist up, but never full-on wiener. I blink a few times and grin. He is beautiful. All of him. But why is he naked? He shouldn't be naked.

Before I can figure it all out, he lays me down and then straddles me. I now have a nude Brandon Levitt on top of me.

He leans in and says in my ear, "Dell, you know you want to."

My head is cloudy. The room is kind of spinning. I can only get one word out. "Taryn?"

"Don't worry, she'll never find out." He breathes heavy in my ear. "I'll make it hot for you. Mooooooooooo." He squeezes my boob. Hard.

I yelp.

1. Because it sort of hurt.
2. It took me completely by surprise. Which sort of
   makes me laugh inside, because when you have

K. M. Walton

a naked guy on top of you, you should not be
surprised when your boob is grabbed.

3. He just mooed in my ear.

"Relax," he says.

I giggle. "Stop." I don't know if I said that out loud or just thought it. A whole bunch of stuff is running through my head. I've never been in a bed with a naked guy. I've liked Brandon for a long time, probably because he was nice to me. This doesn't feel right, though—he loves when I moo in his face. But he's naked. On top of me. And grabbing my boob.

He leans down and kisses me. All 286 pounds of me melts into the daisies. I don't want him to stop. Brandon is a good kisser—tender, not too much tongue—and he keeps his spit in his own mouth. As he's kissing me his hands are doing all kinds of things. One is up underneath my shirt trying to unhook my bra, while the other unbuttons and unzips my jeans. I am amazed at his multitalented hands.

He laughs and snorts. "I can't believe I'm doing this," he says to himself.

He thinks this is a joke. He doesn't want me. A rush of heat floods to my chest, and I can't catch my breath. My hands are glued to my sides like terrified children afraid to pull away from

their mommy. In one long exhale I say, "PleasestopBrandon."
I heard my voice that time. I don't want to do this.

Brandon takes my hands from my sides and places them on his naked back. I'm too scared to move my arms, even a centimeter.

"Touch me."

I shake my head and instantly regret it. Everything goes double. Even him.

"Come on, Dell, touch me," he demands.

I close my eyes to clear my vision. I can't do this. I feel like I'm on a broken merry-go-round whizzing and spinning out of control. I try to sit up. His arm blocks me. Brandon grabs my hand and puts it on his penis. I yank it back, my elbow jamming into his chest. "Ow!" he shouts. Then he leans down. "Let me put it in."

My mouth and brain aren't connected right now. My drunkenness has stolen my voice. Inside my head I say, "Don't want to. Please stop."

Brandon pulls my jeans down from the ankles. *He can't see me naked. I'm too fat.* The room is suddenly plunged into darkness. The music from downstairs seems louder in the dark. My eyes take a few seconds to adjust. I've missed my opportunity to sit up. To get out of this room. Brandon straddles me again.

"I want to go," I say out loud.

K. M. Walton

In one snap, he undoes my bra, and my boobs are freed. He squeezes them both. I try to push him off me, but it is like trying to move a car. I bite my lip and close my eyes. I'm falling, falling, falling.

And shattering.

Then he pulls my underwear down and says, "Stay still." Just like that, he's inside me. I squeeze my legs closed because it hurts.

He scolds me like I'm a child. "Dell, stop!"

Brandon jerks a few times, and then his body goes stiff.

He pulls out and rolls over on his back, panting and wiping his forehead with the back of his hand. "I told you to stop," he says nonchalantly.

Tears roll down my temples into my hair. I have nothing to say. I make no move to cover my nakedness. I lay there like a blob of inhuman matter. I close my eyes, take a deep breath, and do everything in my power to smell the "perfect love smell" of my little sister. I need to smell love right now. It doesn't work, because it never works, and all I smell is sweat.

Brandon is fully dressed and standing at the door. He turns around and says, "Don't tell anyone. This never happened."

The corner of the room gets light for a second as he leaves, and then it goes dark again. I am alone with the daisies.

Bitter Acid Burns

CARA SPENT THE NIGHT DANCING AND TALKING—
not drinking, so she drives home. I say nothing to Cara about
what happened with Brandon. If I open my mouth, I'm going
to vomit. I grip the car door handle to steady my spinning
head and let her go on and on about how much fun she had
dancing. She didn't even realize that I'd disappeared for twenty
minutes. How could she not notice? I would've known if she'd
up and vanished at a party.

I am home by eleven, and my mother is in her bedroom
with the door closed, watching the news. I knock to let her
know I'm back on time. "Good night, Adele," she calls over

the drone of the news. Just once I wish she would invite me in. I'd sprawl across her bed, and we would talk about my night. But this never happens.

"Good night," I call back. It's probably better she keeps her door closed. I don't want to see her pill bottles scattered everywhere, and I'm sure she doesn't want to smell the beer on my breath. I try my best to be quiet in the kitchen, but I bang into just about everything. My mother never comes out. I make myself a huge ham-and-cheese sandwich. It's so thick I can barely get my mouth around it. But I do.

Then I make myself a second sandwich. I am slowly starting to feel un-hollow. And way more sober.

I open the freezer to grab an ice-cream bar, because I can never eat something like a sandwich without finishing it off with something sweet. The cold fog hits my face, and I inhale it, filling my lungs. I close my eyes. Images of bouncing red cups, exploding beer cans, and sex I didn't want to have invade my head. I suck in a second, deeper breath. It would be nice if the cold would deaden the memories of the night. I want to slam the freezer door shut with all of my might, but that would wake everyone up. Instead, I take two bars and gently close the freezer.

I sit down at the table, rip open the first package, and take an enormous bite. Flakes of chocolate coating land on my lap.

I don't bother to brush them away. As I open my mouth to take a second bite, I gag. As far as gags go, it's a decent one. Bitter acid burns the back of my throat.

I barely make it to the toilet before everything comes up. And I do mean everything. I swear there are pieces of my heart in there too. All covered in vomit.

How could I have let Brandon do that to me?

I crawl into bed, trying not to wake up Meggie. I stare at the ceiling, and thoughts start slamming into one another. I am no longer a virgin. I had sex. I didn't want to. Was I raped? Isn't rape, like, violent and forceful, with blood and anger? Could I have really stopped him? Did I try hard enough? He didn't even put a condom on. What if I'm pregnant? Oh my God. Maybe I wanted it. I had a guy's penis inside of me. Someone else's guy.

Sex is a rite of passage—that's what my seventh-grade health teacher told us—and Brandon stole that from me. I wince. He saw me naked. He squeezed my boobs. I'd told him to stop.

I can't tell my mother. We don't know how to talk to each other anymore. Our brief exchanges fall apart pretty quickly these days. My stomach clenches as I imagine how that conversation would go.

Me: Mom, I got wasted at a party and some guy held me down and had sex with me.

Mom: Pass me my pills.

I should tell Cara. I look at my phone but make no effort to reach for it. I can't do it. What just happened to me at Melissa's party is something I should *want* to tell my best friend, but I don't. I mean, I've had forced sex with a very popular guy; I should tell someone. The thing is, I know telling anyone would be social suicide. Even Cara.

I punch the mattress. I think that was rape. Why am I not crying or something? I grab my phone and then drop it onto my chest. I can't even watch magic.

With my stomach empty, I feel hollowed out, a pumpkin scraped of its gooey insides. I squeeze my eyes shut.

I want to lay in the darkness forever.

The apartment is quiet when I wake up Sunday morning. I can't believe I actually fell asleep. It must've been the beer. My eyes examine the water-stained ceiling as I take stock of last night. Nothing has changed. I was drunk. Brandon knew it. I was raped. Brandon's last words—*Don't tell anyone. This never happened*—ache in my head. I wonder how we will act the next time we see each other.

I curl into the fetal position and listen to the birds. Their peppy chirping captivates me, because happiness and its trappings remain a dark mystery. I palm my head and run my fingers through my hair. My skin hurts. *I was raped and I can't tell anyone.* I cover my ears because the birds annoy me now. My brain can no longer appreciate the good and the beautiful—it's too busy cranking out shame and misery.

Eventually, Meggie's demands to get out of her crib snap me out of my pity party. She pads behind me, dragging her blanket, as we walk into the kitchen. I see the note from my mother immediately. It's lying next to my abandoned ice-cream bar.

Adele:

This waste makes me angry.
We are not made of money.
Please clean the toilet today.
It's disgusting.

I crumple her note, grab the now-liquid ice-cream bar, and throw them both in the trash, where they belong. The morning disappears in a mixture of television, science research, eating, and toilet cleaning. I print out my project during Meggie's nap. I got permission to write a research paper because I didn't want to ask my mother for money to buy new materials. I did the bare minimum just to get it done, and it shows. My paper's only two pages. Who cares? I seriously don't.

The first word Meggie utters after her nap is "park." We both chow down some lunch and head to the good park, the one just past school. I walk on autopilot. Then I hear the familiar crack of a bat as it makes contact with the ball. I stop dead on the sidewalk. The softball field is right on the other side of the chain-link fence and is covered with recognizable blue-and-white uniforms. *What is the matter with me? Why would I come this way? Half of my team has spotted me. Damnit, damnit, damnit.*

In order to get this over with, I drop my head and pick up my pace. Despite this genius plan, I am one hundred percent un-missable.

I sneak a glance at home plate just as the catcher springs into action to rescue a wild pitch. She throws it back to our pitcher, and then our eyes briefly meet. My stomach flips. I half expect her to wave or acknowledge me, but she doesn't. As I pass the pitching mound, I listen for someone to shout hello. Only traffic noises from the passing cars and the *click-clack* of Meggie's stroller wheels fill the air. The entire team watched me walk by—I know they did. Unbelievable.

I take a right at the STOP sign so I can distance myself from the field. I don't want to be near them.

Each step I take pushes softball further into my past. From behind I hear another crack of the bat—the hit was huge, I can tell—but I have no desire to turn around. I walk away from the field, away from a team that barely accepted me. I wait at the light, staring down at the top of Meggie's little head. A sniff of love is exactly what I need right now.

I'm bent over, inhaling my sister's perfect smell, when it dawns on me—I don't miss softball. It was never *my* passion. And the fact I'm not longing to play or boo-hooing over getting cut proves that it's over. In fact, I'd like to dig a hole in the ground and bury softball. There's a ton of other crap I'd like to throw in that hole too: Brandon, DD, my mother's pills. I'd fill the hole with dirt, pat it down with my bare hands, maybe even hum a tune while doing so. Then I'd dance on top.

As Meggie plays in the sandbox, I text Cara. I've sent her four messages, but so far, no response. The brief bit of peace I felt from Meggie's smell and letting softball go is long gone. I am in full-on panic mode. I'm worrying that our friendship is over, that she has replaced me with the jumping girls. Or that she somehow found out about what happened with Brandon. I rummage through Meggie's diaper bag and grab every snack I can find: a teething cookie, toddler fruit snacks, a squished oatmeal bar. I swallow the last tasteless bite of oatmeal bar, reach for the bag, and in an effort to find more food, haphazardly pile the contents next to me. I've eaten everything. But I find an old pair of sunglasses and put them on. I can feel the tear factory gearing up.

Of course I've lost Cara to the jumping girls. I don't fit in and she does. Shit, who am I kidding? I don't fit in *anywhere* or in any*thing*. Maybe if I go on a diet and lose weight, she'll act like my best friend again. But the problem is, imagining Cara and I skipping off into the sunset, chanting "Best Friends Forever!" is not only stupid, it's unrealistic.

But mostly, it's stupid.

The Ugly, Ugly Walk

I'M IN BED WHEN I TEXT CARA ONE MORE TIME:

> You okay? I'm worried.

No response.

I can't fall asleep, so I try watching some magic videos. They're not helping, and I turn off my phone. My eyes are heavy, but my thoughts won't let me sleep. I toss and turn for what feels like hours, trying to get comfortable, trying to quiet my head.

I give up and stare. Sometime after four in the morning

I conclude that sleep won't help me, it won't stop my pain. I should just stay awake and feel the hurt. I let it weigh on me. Holding me down. It's a bottomless, heavy ache, so deep I swear it's in my bones.

I turn my phone on before dragging myself out of bed, and I see that Cara finally texted me back. I read her text ten thousand times:

Phone died. I am sorry, Dell.

Her phone never dies.

I fixate on the "I am sorry, Dell." It's so final. There's nothing to respond to. No opening or invitation to text her back, so I don't. And she was sorry about what exactly? Her phone dying? Was she apologizing for something else? I devise every possible scenario, each of which crumbles to dust, leaving only one option: She ditched me for Sydney and her friends.

My mother calls from the kitchen, "Adele, get in the shower!

I zombie-walk to the bathroom to get ready for school.

With my towel wrapped around me, I stare into my closet. It's full of clothes, but I've never worn most of them. I reach up, ruffle the tags, and shake my head. I grab my usual jeans and T-shirt. My bed squeaks underneath my weight as I sprawl across it. This routine of sucking my gut in so my zipper goes up starts my days with heaping servings of self-loathing. Every morning begins with a: "Good morning, Adele, you beast."

I check my phone for new texts from Cara. Nothing. I do a few twists and turns in the mirror and cringe.

Meggie's voice makes me jump. "Dehwy? Get out?"

I smile. I really don't want to smile, but I can't help it. She is too cute. I walk over to my sister's crib. "Good morning, Meggie-bideggie." Her curly brown hair is adorable. It's bouncy and shiny and compliments her big brown eyes.

Meggie throws her arms out, and I pick her up. My little sister and her blanket come out of the crib as one unit, as usual.

"You love your blankie, don't you, Megs?" She nods. "Okay, I gotta go, girl. Come on." Meggie nuzzles her warm head into my neck. She wraps her little arms and legs around me. I rub my lips on her baby-soft hair and breathe her in as I carry her into the kitchen. When I go to put her into her high chair, she clings tighter. I hug her back and whisper, "Love you too."

"Again, Adele?" my mother barks, looking me up and down. "Are you wearing the same jeans? My God, your grandmother spent hundreds of dollars on clothes for you, and you wear a grubby *Simpsons* T-shirt?"

I am in no mood to argue with her. I don't have the energy. "Happy Monday morning to you, Mother." I stare at her. She used to look good in the morning. Fresh and smiley. She can't seem to muster up pretty—or happy, for that matter. She only looks dull or really dull.

"You have a closet full of clothes I've never seen you wear! I don't get you."

I mumble under my breath, "Yeah, I know."

"What? Stop talking with marbles in your mouth."

I sit at the table and push my sliced strawberries through my cottage cheese. I know my mother is watching, so I rearrange the fruit without eating.

"I'm trying to help you, Adele," my mother says. God, she looks wiped out. She must not have slept again last night.

"Stop trying," is all I can say.

The walk to school is an ugly, ugly walk. My thoughts are so heavy, I don't know how my feet aren't sunk into the sidewalk. A few times I stop and lean against a tree, just to calm down. What if everyone knows what Brandon did to me? That he thought it was some kind of a joke?

I see Cara up ahead at our usual spot out front, but she's standing with Emma and Melissa. I'm out of breath and sweaty when I reach them. "H-hey." Cara and Emma share a series of quick looks and an outbreak of laughter. This behavior cements what I already suspect: Cara was out with them yesterday and chose to ignore my texts.

"Dell, did you see us dancing at the party?" Cara asks with an over-the-top smile. I've seen that smile before. In fact, I know it well. It's the same fake smile we practiced in eighth grade, imitating the popular girls—namely, Taryn—to make ourselves laugh. I break eye contact with her mouth and study the rest of her face for signs that she's joking. I don't know, I think she's trying to impress Emma and Melissa.

I nod in response to Cara's question, so I don't sound all breathy, and sit down on the wall. I'd like to ask Cara a million things, but questioning her about why she didn't call me yesterday would make me look like a fool, like a pesky, needy dweeb. *Where were you, Cara? Do you still like me, Cara? Are you still my best friend, Cara? Why did it take you so long to text me back, Cara?*

I play it cool, put my earbuds in, and pretend I'm listening to music. I watch Cara and the other two girls. They're just so pretty, all three of them. Me? I look like I just ate three pretty girls for breakfast.

Buses drop off hordes of kids, and everyone congregates on the front walkway and grass. I spy Chase and Jacob the table-lifter and watch them playfully shove their way to the hill. If they're here that means Brandon can't be too far behind. I slump down in my best retreating-turtle imitation and wish myself invisible. I know I'll have to see him eventually, but the thought of interacting with him right now cracks my heart straight down the middle and just might kill me. Then everyone would have to step over my dead body on their way into school.

Cara turns to Emma. "Oh my God, Em, my legs are killing me."

Em? She's calling her Em?

Emma and Melissa squeal back at the same time, "Me toooooooo!"

Melissa stares at me for a second, then pulls Cara and Emma in toward her. "She can't hear us, right?"

I move my head to the imaginary music. Cara and Emma both turn to look over at me. Even if I actually *were* listening to blaring music, I would've been able to tell they were about to talk about me or say something they didn't want me to hear. Heat surges to my face.

"Like Taryn said before, Dell is too big to run anywhere. It would be so embarrassing if anyone saw us with her. You know?" Melissa snickers. "So let's run that same trail next Sunday," she says. "Maybe we can get Taryn to come too." Cara and Emma nod.

Cara isn't coming to my defense. Her nod, agreeing with what Melissa just said about me, burns and chars my heart. It's a pile of black dust.

And shit, they *were* together. They were off having fun while I stuffed my face with toddler snacks, reliving what happened on the daisy quilt.

Taryn and Sydney stroll over. With each step they take, I silently plead: *Please don't let Taryn know about what happened with Brandon.* They glance at me for a second before joining the other girls and turning their backs to me. I don't think they realize I was technically "with" Cara, Emma, and Melissa.

"Show them," Taryn demands. Sydney pulls her hair back to reveal a whopping hickey. The five girls exchange grins. I play with my phone.

"Slut," Taryn says. Everyone laughs. "While I'm stuck talking to my fat cousin all night, she was having her neck sucked by Chase, and you guys were having fun dancing without me. Brandon said the party sucked because he missed me so much."

There's a chorus of "awwwws."

I drop my chin to my chest. Brandon is a lying prick. I rock back and forth, pretending to jam out, but in reality I'm pretty close to *passing* out. The motion is helping me stay upright.

Taryn clearly has something else to say from the smirk on her face. She smoothes her hair as they all lean in. "Brandon told me he loved me last night."

My leg jerks and kicks over my backpack, spilling the contents of the front pocket. Pencils roll all over the sidewalk. "Shit." I yank my earbuds out.

As if their heads are pulled by an invisible puppet string, the girls all turn to look at me in unison.

"Are you eavesdropping on us, Dell?" Taryn asks. "Because if you are, that's, like, middle-school shit."

I ignore her and retrieve my pencils. Some have rolled into the street, and I leave them.

The warning bell rings. Taryn, Melissa, Emma, and Sydney lock arms. Emma holds an arm out for Cara. For a split second I think Cara is going to follow them down the yellow brick road, but she doesn't. "I'll see you guys in there. I have to talk to her."

The girls stay linked as they make their way up the stairs, and they don't break apart when they reach the door. Taryn opens it, and they follow her in single file, still connected. Cara hasn't taken her eyes from them, and she chuckles at their theatrics.

She turns to look at me. It's just the two of us now. She squints. "Dell, where did you disappear to at the party?"

Perfection, Maybe?

"NOWHERE," I SAY.

Cara stares suspiciously and crosses her arms. "Dell, Sydney said she saw you go upstairs with Brandon. Is that true?"

Shit. Sydney saw me with Brandon, which means Taryn will find out, because they all tell her everything. Which means everyone will suspect something happened between Brandon and me. If they think we hooked up, I'll be public enemy number one.

I say, with as much nonchalance as I can muster, "He wanted to show me some stupid video on YouTube. It was no big deal." I pinch my eyebrows together. I can't believe the words "no big deal" just exited my mouth.

"Yeah, well, if Taryn finds out that you were alone with her boyfriend, we'll never get invited to another party. As in never ever. You shouldn't have gone upstairs with him, Dell."

Her tone is so harsh. If she's freaking out about me going upstairs to watch a video with Brandon, she would go ape-shit if she knew we had sex. I can't tell her. She would definitely leave me in the dust.

"You are going to ruin everything." She finishes with a long, breathy exhale.

I look away and whisper, "Sorry."

More dramatic air exits her nose. "You should be."

We part ways and head to our lockers.

Brandon and Taryn are at the end of the hallway. He has her skinny little body pinned up against the lockers and is kissing her neck. He turns his head, sees me, and pauses—midkiss—and stares.

His look speaks volumes: *Keep your mouth shut, fat girl.*

If I had an ax, I'd love to hold him down and chop his nuts off. Or if I had the guts, give him the finger. But I busy myself in my locker. By the time I slam it shut, they're long gone. I've broken out in a cold sweat. My T-shirt clings to my stomach and back. A single bead of panic rolls down my spine, tickling my skin like a spider. I shiver as I round the corner.

If I tell anyone about the rape, I risk major backlash. People won't believe that Brandon raped me. I know it.

I take my seat in English, and Sydney sits right behind me. "Hey, Dell, fun party, right?"

I don't want to make eye contact with her, so I stay facing forward. "Sure. Yeah." Sydney taps my shoulder. I grit my teeth and turn around.

"Why did you go upstairs with Brandon?"

I can feel my face go red. "To watch a video."

"Uh-huh. Right." She gives me a sly grin.

"What are you trying to say?" I ask her.

She leans in and whispers, "You were gone for, like, a half hour. And Brandon seemed . . ." Her voice trails off.

"Seemed what?"

"Um, well, he seemed pretty sweaty when he came back down."

I roll my eyes to act all casual and whatever-ish, but my insides are on fire. Like, I may burn to the ground. I'm about to babble some excuse, paint some phony picture for her, but I don't. If this shit goes viral, then it's all over anyway. I might as well move to another planet, because no sumo-wrestler impersonation or self-deprecating joke will save me from the onslaught.

They will eat me alive. And what a feast I'd be. I'd feed everyone.

Sydney continues in a hushed tone, "Don't worry, I won't tell Taryn. She wants to dump him anyway. She's got the hots for Jacob Unger." Her hand flies up to cover her mouth. "Shit, Dell. Don't tell her I told you that."

Sydney is the Fort Knox of secret-keepers.

Jacob? The table-lifter? He's a dick. He and Taryn *would* make the ideal couple.

My teacher, Mrs. Salvatore, starts class, and I am relieved of having to look at Sydney's stupid face.

I fluff my way through the rest of the day, which is unlike me. I usually raise my hand, participate, answer questions. Not today. I spend my time worrying that Sydney will start an avalanche of rumors by sharing what she thinks went on upstairs at the party. If she knew the truth—that I was raped by a guy who gets a kick out of making me moo like a cow—her head might burst.

Other than Sydney, no one else says anything about the party. I pray Sydney will keep her mouth shut like she said she would. Somewhere during the afternoon, my thoughts turn angry. I can't believe *I'm* feeling nervous and ashamed. I didn't do anything wrong.

The cherry on top of my fuming-mad sundae? After my last class, two of my old teammates walk by me, like, two feet away, and don't even say hi. I actually snort. I don't care. I never liked any of them. I don't miss them. They can all go directly to hell.

I stand at my open locker, put my earbuds in, and blast music for real this time. I feel a tap on my shoulder. It's Cara. She always meets me at my locker after the last bell, but it surprises me after the way she acted this morning. I don't take my earbuds out, and I just stare at her. I'm still in a crap mood. I can't take another accusatory line of questioning. I might crack and tell her the truth.

Without saying a word, she links her arm in mine and leads me down the hall. Maybe this is her way of apologizing. I feel my feet moving, and I know I am walking, but I'm not paying attention to where we're going. I keep my gaze glued to the floor because I do not want to see Brandon. Cara stops, yanks an earbud out of my ear, and says, "Well?"

I tilt my head to the side. "Well, what?"

"Well aren't you going to yell at me? Make a face? Anything?"

I yank out my other earbud. "Cara, I don't know what the hell you're talking about." It is then that I hear the saxophone and register where I am. Cara has dragged me to the auditorium. More specifically, to the talent show tryouts.

"Why am I here, Cara?"

"You know."

"I know nothing."

K. M. Walton

"Well, I know that you have an amazing voice. Why are you acting so weird today? You're like a zombie," she says. "Is it because of what I said this morning? All I meant was that we have to be careful or, you know, we won't get to go to anymore parties. I didn't mean to yell at you or anything."

I nod slowly. I think she just apologized to me, but I'm not sure. However, I *am* sure that I'm not getting onstage. "Cara, I am not, repeat not, trying out for the talent show. Period. End of story."

"I already signed you up. You're singing the Sarah McLachlan song about the angel. Get over it."

"You shouldn't have done that." I am not in the mood to be around people, let alone in front of an audience. Not today.

"What? I shouldn't look out for my best friend? Give you the chance to share your voice with the world? Oh, poor, poor Dell. My-life-sucks Dell. I'm-just-going-to-boo-hoo-through-the-rest-of-my-junior-year-feeling-sorry-for-myself Dell. Suck it up. Life blows sometimes. It happens to everyone. This will be good for you. You are going to try out, and you are going to make it. And you are going to amaze everyone with your talent." Then she adds, in a full-on-imitation of me, "Period. End of story. Good night. The end."

She called me her best friend. Those words twinkle like stars in the darkness.

I guess she told me.

I guess I'm trying out for the talent show.

I guess I have as good a shot as anyone else here.

I guess Cara has slightly redeemed herself as my best friend.

I guess I'm going to need something to wear if I make it.

Someone announces that it's my turn to try out. I take a deep breath and make my way to the stage. I *guess* I'm doing this. I'm about to start singing a capella, when music comes from the speakers. Cara must've given them a karaoke version. I open and close my hands as I wait for my entry point. And I sing. I'm into the second verse when the strangest sensation starts in my fingers. It's not bad, just weird, like tingling. It travels up my arms and settles in behind my face. Maybe the sensation is confidence, I don't know. But I feel different.

I want to reach out and wrap my hands around the microphone, maybe even sway my hips to the music. I wish I could get into my performance—yank the microphone out of the stand, toss my hair around, fall to my knees. You know, like the divas do in their videos.

I don't, though.

In the audience, Cara's mouthing the words along with me, and after each line she gestures for me to smile. It's weird, but I want to smile, so I do. It's like the smile releases my voice, because it goes louder and sounds even more powerful. I belt it out.

I come to the big finish and throw my head back, letting the last few words barrel out of me like a herd of elephants.

I beam. Cara's clapping and jumping up and down. I forgive her for being bitchy this morning. Everyone else is cheering, and my smile widens so much it hurts. I can't seem to think of any words to describe it.

Perfection, maybe.

You'll Figure It Out. Right.

I DO MY MATH HOMEWORK AT THE KITCHEN TABLE. The apartment is silent except for the crunch of potato chips in my mouth. The only sound is my rhythmic chewing. I pick up the bag and read the nutrition information. "Twelve chips. Who eats twelve chips?" Whoever decides official serving sizes of food must have the appetite of a bird.

Brandon's voice fills my head. *This never happened. Don't tell anyone.* My leg bounces underneath the table. I think the part that hurts the most was how he laughed just before saying, *I can't believe I'm doing this.* I swear I can still feel the warmth of his breath on my shoulder, like tattooed disgrace.

I'm finally crying. No, I'm dripping humiliation. I reach up and wipe my cheeks. What an asshole. I want to push Brandon down a flight of stairs and have him smash into pieces at the bottom. I want him so broken that he's unrecognizable. Unable to hold any other girl down and tell her to "stay still."

With a shaking hand, I reach into the bag of chips. Each handful fills my mouth with greasy, salty calm.

The bag is gone.

What else do I want? A sandwich, maybe? As I layer ham on cheese, I force myself to think of good things, like I'm pretty sure that I nailed my audition. Actually, I'm excited to see the talent show list tomorrow morning, which is funny, because if someone had told me yesterday that I would care about this list, I think I'd have laughed in their face. Maybe even added a knee slap.

But I want to make it.

I swallow my last bite of sandwich and allow the food to fill up every empty space. A deep sense of calm settles over me. I feel safe. And as I sit in my food-induced peace, it comes to me—I know why I care. When I was up onstage, I got lost in the moment. My voice filled the auditorium. No one mooed. No one made an inappropriate joke or sound of any kind. After I finished, everyone in the auditorium clapped and hooted.

Standing onstage, with people cheering for me, filled me with so much contentment, even more than any bag of chips or sandwich could. I overflowed like a pot of spaghetti, bubbling with intensity, boiling over the stage. That was me. An intense, boiling pot of spaghetti.

I literally run into Brandon as I'm rounding the corner on my way to lunch. As in, I knock him down and he lands flat on his ass. I burst into nervous laughter.

This pisses him off. "Dude! What's your problem?" He pulls himself up and scowls, glancing around to see if anyone saw him crash into the Adele-wall. The hallway is almost empty because the bell already rang, which is why I was hurrying in the first place. I'm late. To lunch. My favorite period.

"I didn't do it on purpose, Brandon."

He takes off his baseball hat, runs his hands through his hair, and puts the hat back on. "I have a game today."

I have no idea what that has to do with anything. "Huh?"

Looking through me, he says, "I have a game, and I don't need any injuries effing it up. Scouts are coming today."

"Oh." I feel small right now. Like a flea on a rat. And the rat is Brandon Levitt.

He jogs down the hall, ending our first post-sex conversation. Clearly he wants to forget what he did. Clearly he has no

K. M. Walton

intention of apologizing. Clearly he wants nothing to do with me. Clearly he is a total dick.

This hollows me out again. Air and life have left my body. I'm empty. I don't know how I'm standing. I should be a big pile of flesh—a misshapen mound of skin in everyone's way—needing to be shoveled into a trash bag and thrown into the Dumpster behind the school. By two people.

I somehow make it to the cafeteria and Cara plops down next to me with her usual salad. "They haven't posted the list yet. I just checked."

I'm in midchew so I nod. I want to believe everything is back to normal between us. She's definitely acting regular right now. But I wonder if Cara would still sit with me if Sydney or her friends were in this lunch period. I imagine me sitting alone with my tray while Cara sits with her skinny, gorgeous new friends.

My eye twitches in reaction to my vision-o-awful, and I cringe.

"Stop making faces, Dell. I know you made it. I don't know about me. That freshman kid may have beaten me. Do you think they'd have two piano players?" She looks down at my tray. "What are you eating?"

"You were way better than him, Cara. And it's called a salad." If I make it into the talent show, I'll need a cute dress, so I decided to go on a diet. I should try and drop, oh, I don't know, like, a hundred and fifty pounds so I look normal onstage.

"Salad? Since when do you eat salad?" She rolls her eyes. "Wait. Are you on a diet? I can't believe you didn't tell me. You think you're getting in, don't you?" She takes a sip of her water bottle. "It's a good idea, and even if I don't get in, I want to go shopping with you, because you are so getting in."

That was a one-sided conversation. I do kind of think I'm getting in, but I still say, "You don't know that."

"Are we doing this again? This 'what I know versus what you know' shit? Because listen closely, Dell, you are in. I know it. You blew the roof off the auditorium. Your eyes sparkled like diamonds up there. You should've heard what kids were saying out in the audience. Melissa was freaking out."

I felt it. I saw it. I still like to hear Cara say it. Somehow it makes it even more real. I shrug.

"Deny it all you want, people were going nuts, Dell. Melissa kept asking me if I knew you could sing like that. I swear I saw Mrs. Salvatore wipe away a tear. Don't even act like you don't know you made it. Puh-leeze." She takes a bite of her salad. "You owe me."

"Oh, okay. Right. So I owe you for sneaking behind my back and signing me up for something I didn't want to do

K. M. Walton

in the first place?" I'm just messing with her. I'm glad Cara pushed me. I wouldn't have auditioned unless she did what she did.

Cara grins and pelts my shoulder with a cherry tomato. "You bitch."

I stick my tongue out at her and go back to eating. My eyes wander from my tray to Cara's. *My* salad is covered with ranch. There's no green showing at all. It's all white. My lettuce is drowning in dressing, but it still has to be fewer calories and less fat than my typical double cheeseburger, large cheese fries, and large soda. Maybe I'll just starve myself. I must have enough body fat to keep me alive for at least a year.

"When do you want to go shopping?" she asks. "Since you don't have softball practice anymore, we could go right after school."

Shopping is awful.

I haven't shopped for clothes with Cara since I gained the last forty pounds. And the last time we did, it was a catastrophe. That was when I found out that the clothes in regular shops no longer fit me. The stores we usually went to only went up to size sixteen. I tried stuffing myself into size-sixteen jeans for at least five minutes. After I'd accidentally busted the zipper and was hiding the pants in the rack, Cara popped out of her dressing room, asking if her jeans (size six) made her butt look

empty

big. I had to bite the inside of my cheek to keep from crying.

I tasted blood for ten minutes straight.

I swallowed the bitter iron taste in my mouth and admitted that nothing fit me. Cara tried to help by suggesting we see if Large and Lovely had anything cute. Large and Lovely is the shop we *used* to walk by, giggle, and call the "Fat Lady Store." I faked stomach cramps and went home. Now I avoid clothing stores whenever we hit the mall and put my full concentration on the food court.

"I don't know. What would I do with Meggie?"

"Isn't Meggie at day care?" Cara asks.

My stomach bottoms out. I can't go dress shopping with her. I have to get out of this. "Yeah, but I can't be late picking her up. We'd only have, like, twenty minutes to shop by the time we got to the mall. My mom gets charged two bucks for every minute I'm late. It'll be a hassle."

"Dell!" Cara hits the table with her closed fist. "This is important!"

"Relax."

"You're not going onstage in a T-shirt and jeans. Seriously," she says.

"I know. God, you are a pain in my ass. I'll figure it out."

Figure what out? the voice in my head antagonizes. *You're not going shopping. You're dropping out of the show. You have no nice clothes that fit you. Your mother works two jobs and spends any leftover money on diapers and pills. Your father's extra coin goes directly to the one and only Donna Dumbass. You have no money. You are enormous. But you'll figure it out.*

Right.

Letting Go of the Rope

IF LUNCH IS MY FAVORITE SUBJECT, YOU'D FULLY expect that phys ed would be the fat girl's nemesis. It is, but it's not because I'm unathletic (I could probably *out*-athletic 80 percent of the guys in my class); it's the changing for gym and getting undressed part that makes me want to throw on an invisibility cloak. Taryn and Sydney are in my gym class, and so is my former teammate Amy. And having anyone—especially those three—see me without my clothes on isn't going to happen.

I've developed a system for the days I have gym. I wear my gym shorts all day, then I dart to the locker room like a lunatic so I can throw on my T-shirt before everyone else arrives, then wait on the bleachers for all of the slow/skinny people.

Darting anywhere is difficult, so I'm sitting and panting when Coach Lein walks into the gym with a bundle of rope over his shoulder. "A little help, Turner."

Together we unwind the rope and lay it in a straight line. He tells me we're doing tug-of-war today. I nod and sit back down as relief floods my brain. Despite my athleticism, I hate when class involves running of any kind. I'm sure the reason is glaringly obvious.

Kids trickle into the gym. Sydney and Taryn strut across the gym floor. They're like salt and pepper shakers—one with bright blond hair, the other with jet-black. Both have rolled up their shorts so much that if they bent over, we'd all get an ass show. Taryn is petting her hair while Sydney arranges her T-shirt so a bit of her stomach shows. They stand off to the side and ignore everyone but each other.

Coach Lein blows his whistle. He announces the plan for the class and picks Amy and some guy with the hairiest arms and legs on the planet to choose tug-of-war teams. Ape-man chooses Taryn and Sydney right out of the gate. He probably has a boner for both of them. Amy chooses one of the football players and one of the flip-cup guys from the baseball team. She's going for strength.

They go back and forth, choosing their teams, and I look around. There are only three of us left. I want that cloak right now.

"I've gotta grab the stopwatch from my office," Coach Lein says. He jogs off.

"I want Dell," Amy announces.

Taryn and Sydney snort. "Cows *are* strong," Taryn says loudly.

"I want to win, beauty queen!" Amy yells back.

Amy waves me over. For a split second I fear my feet won't get me there—the embarrassment seems to have temporarily frozen me. But when I drop my gaze to the floor, my body moves.

Coach Lein returns and starts shouting commands. Amy puts me at the end of our rope. I figured she would. I'm bigger than the football guy. Coach goes through the rules, then yells, "Go!"

I barely grip the rope because I don't care about winning or getting a good grade in this exercise. I get jerked forward a bit. The football guy is right in front of me. He looks over his shoulder and barks, "Do something!" Oh, I want to do *something,* all right. *How about my foot slips and kicks you in the nuts?*

The gym fills with voices bellowing, "Pull!" Then Taryn's voice cuts through. "Moooooo! Mooooooo!"

I let go of the rope.

My team stumbles forward, everyone tripping into one another while the other team falls back on their butts. Apparently I was doing more pulling than I'd thought.

Sydney lands on top of Taryn, and they laugh like hyenas. Amy is in my face, asking me why I let go. The football dude is shaking his head.

I let my shoulders answer for me, and I look away.

The next morning there is a hand-drawn picture of a cow taped to my locker. BEWARE OF THE RAPIST BOVINE is neatly bubble-lettered underneath. I rip it off, crumple it up, and look around for who did it. Everyone seems to be minding their own business. *How many people have already seen this?* My mouth goes dry.

On my way to homeroom, I regroup in a bathroom stall. I un-crinkle the page and stare at it. The cow is so fat. The lettering is girly. I shake my head, hoping it will erase the image like an Etch A Sketch. I feel light-headed when I get still.

I'll bet Sydney wrote it. She's the only one who suspects that anything happened.

Unless.

Unless Sydney told everyone. What if everyone knows that I had sex with Taryn's boyfriend? What if Taryn knows?

I lean my forehead against the stall. I can feel blood draining to my feet, see tiny white stars twinkling in my line of vision.

Don't faint, Adele. You'll get stuck in some effed-up angle and they'll have to use the Jaws of Life to get you out of the stall.

Somebody is trying to make me squirm. But *I* didn't rape *him*. What the hell does this stupid drawing even mean?

I crush the paper into a ball again. I have to get to homeroom or I'll get a detention. A detention means I can't pick up Meggie. And that means a pissed-off mother.

I manage to slip into the classroom and take my seat just as the bell rings. The principal comes over the loudspeaker with the announcements. No one ever listens to her, so I don't even know why the woman bothers. Everyone just gossips and rushes to finish homework. One word slices through the morning chatter that makes me listen: talent. I stare at the speaker above the whiteboard. The talent show list has been posted on the auditorium doors, and whoever tried out is allowed out of homeroom to check. My body relaxes, and I slump back down. I don't care anymore. That cow drawing officially pulled a black cloud over me.

Someone knocks at the door. Cara waves at me through the glass. I shake my head. She jumps up and down a few times and beckons me again. Now everyone is looking at me. My teacher nods as I grab my backpack and silently walk out.

Cara squeals, "Oh my God, Dell, hurry up! Let's go!"

I close the door behind me. "I don't want to do this anymore."

"Well, you sort of already tried out. So let's go." Cara drags me down the hallway. I'm numb.

There's a crowd surrounding the list, so we can't get close enough to read it. Cara squeezes my arm. She pushes her way to the front. After a few seconds, her arms shoot up victoriously. *Well, one of us made it.*

She maneuvers her way back through the crowd. When she reaches me, she erupts into full-on squeal-and-jump mode. I swear her head might dislocate from her neck. Cara holds out her arms for a hug. I stare at them.

"Come on, you can't leave me hanging," she whines.

I give her the lamest hug in the history of hugs.

"We both made it!" she shouts. I wish I could feel excited. Performing in the talent show just doesn't matter anymore. I can't silence the screaming demon inside of me: Adele let herself get raped! She is a fat pig who eats her weight in junk food! Her best friend is drifting away from her! She'll be completely alone soon!

The demon is winning.

Cara bounces and then twirls around. "This is awesome! And Melissa is the MC. She'll look so pretty introducing everyone."

I shove my hands deep into my front pockets. Is this why Cara is excited? Because Melissa is involved in the show? From her far-off gaze, I'm leaning toward yes. Cara says dreamily, "I wonder what Melissa will wear." She snaps out of her trance. "This will be good for our image, Dell. You will out-sing everyone, and I will be so proud of you. You know that I am the best friend you'll ever have, right?" Cara rests her head on my shoulder.

She is the *only* friend I'll ever have. Maybe it's the warm pressure of her head against me or the fact that she's acting like my best friend again, but I have a sudden and overwhelming urge to tell her everything: what happened with Brandon, that I know she spent Sunday with those girls, that my father is getting remarried and never coming home, that my heart is having the hardest damn time beating inside my chest because I'm close to fading into the darkness. "I have to tell you—" I abruptly stop.

Cara pulls away and looks at me, waiting for me to continue.

I can't tell her any of that shit. What is the matter with me?

She links her arm into mine. "Tell me what?"

My chest puffs up, and I blurt out the first thing that comes to mind. "I don't want to do this, Cara."

"Do what? Shop? Because guess what, you have no choice, my friend. You are not, repeat not, wearing a T-shirt and jeans onstage."

I don't have the heart to clarify that I'm talking about the show. The tingling happiness I'd felt after tryouts is dead. The demon ate it. Or maybe it was the cow. And the thought of shopping for an outfit to wear while an auditorium full of people stare at me makes me want to lock myself in a closet.

Cara plows onward, babbling about our practice schedule, blissfully unaware of how close I came to spilling my guts. Our friendship would end if I was honest about the rape. She couldn't handle what happened—or knowing who raped me. And who his girlfriend is.

Or the unthinkable could happen: She wouldn't believe me.

Either way I know Cara would abandon me. Popularity is finally in her grasp. Remain friends with the enormous, ugly, fat girl who was raped by the hottest guy in school or become friends with four of the prettiest, skinniest, most fashionable, and popular girls in school?

Truthfully, the choice is obvious. It's sort of like being offered a bowl of shit or a bowl of ice cream.

I know that I have to keep my mouth shut. About everything.

I need space. The crowd thins out, and I seize my opportunity to walk away. I head over to the list so I can see it with my own eyes.

Dell Turner: "Angel" by Sarah McLachlan

I did make it. Cara hugs random people, her face animated with pure exhilaration. My stomach tightens.

My voice sounded great. I liked the cheering. I wanted this.

Me, a rapist cow? The victim? The one who was held down and disgraced?

I can't celebrate. Or smile.

Filled with Dejection

HALFWAY HOME, CARA DROPS HER LET'S-GO-shopping mission and goes back to discussing how "out-of-control awesome" it was that we got invited to Melissa's party the other night. I shut out her voice and contemplate my current situation. Whoever taped that picture to my locker knows I had sex with Brandon. Boys don't usually write in bubble letters. But who did it?

If it was Sydney, I could try and convince her not to tell anyone else. Even though she's not the most trustworthy person, she doesn't have the same venom coursing through her veins as Taryn, and I think I could successfully appeal to her.

If it was Taryn, well, then I'm screwed—she will attack and gouge and rip.

Anger unexpectedly pumps through my veins. That means someone is accusing me of raping Brandon—

Cara squeezes my arm, stopping my deluge of thoughts. "That was like walking home with a piece of wood."

"I know. Sorry. I guess I'm tired."

"I can't believe you're not happy about the talent show, Dell."

"I'm fine."

"'Fine' isn't 'happy,' last time I checked." There's a touch of annoyance in her voice.

"Fine, I'm happy." The side of my mouth lifts into a half grin. I'm trying to show her that I'm good. I'm doing everything in my power to keep my shit together.

Cara mouths a dramatic "Whatever" and continues on her way.

Somewhere along the next three blocks my thoughts jump from anger straight to terror: Taryn Anderson. If Taryn knows about the sex, my miserable life will plunge into the fiery depths of hell. She will verbally tear me to shreds, publicly humiliate me, and do everything in her power to ruin my life. I've seen her do it to other girls—girls who didn't even have sex with her boyfriend.

My hands shake as I unlock my apartment door. I hear a

K. M. Walton

loud *bang* from inside, and I freeze. I'm always the first one home. I have a routine. I used to have practice, come home, shower, eat something, then pick up Meggie at Mrs. McNash's house. Now I just come home from school, eat in front of the TV, and get my sister. My mother is always at work.

Pushing the door open, I stand on the landing like a statue and only let my eyes enter. I'm not stepping a toe in there. There are no masked gunmen in my line of vision, so I listen. Another sound comes from the back of the apartment. I lean my head over the threshold and strain to hear what it is.

Crying.

It is my mother. I am at her bedroom door in seconds. "Mom, hey, are you okay?" I say through the closed door.

She yelps. "Damnit, Adele!"

I guess I should've knocked first or something, but that probably would've scared her too. This isn't my specialty. "Sorry."

My mother sniffles loudly. "Why aren't you at softball? Did you get Megs?" she shouts through the closed door.

I suspect now is not the best time to tell her that I got cut because I'm too fat. I answer her second question instead. "No, not yet."

"Don't," she says.

I squeeze my eyebrows together. Why is my mother telling

me not to get her? Picking up Meggie from day care is my favorite part of my day.

"Did you hear me?" she asks, obviously annoyed.

"May I come in?" I ask. I'm tired of talking to a freaking door.

"Hold on." Then I hear all sorts of rustling and nose blowing. "Come in."

I hesitate, because honestly, I'm not sure what I'm going to find on the other side. She's sitting on the edge of her bed with her head down, hands on her knees. Her nightstand is littered with prescription bottles and half-empty glasses of water.

"What's the matter?" I ask.

Without raising her head, she says, "The drugstore let me go. I got fired, that's what's the matter."

I want to say more, but the only word that leaves my mouth is "Oh."

Now she raises her head. "Oh? That's all you have to say to me? Oh?"

I backtrack. "I'm sorry?"

"Well I'm sorry too, Adele. Without that paycheck we're screwed."

"I'm sorry. I'll get a job to help. We'll make it work." *Where is this optimistic confidence coming from?*

Mom comes at me, and I swear I think she's going to hit

me, so my hands fly up to cover my face. She grabs my forearms. My face contorts. She smacks me in the side of the head. "We're gonna drown! Nothing's gonna work. Your father owes me thirty-four thousand dollars!" she screams. Her eyes are bloodshot from crying, or whatever drug cocktail she's probably swallowed.

I take a step back because I don't want to be in range of a second hit. "Calm down."

Again, I say the wrong thing, because her eyes bulge and she is on me, nose-to-nose. "Don't tell me to calm down," she growls. "You don't know shit, Adele."

I am mute.

I know everything there is to know about shit because I'm covered in it, a regular ol' pig in the sty. I know shit.

Mom retreats to her bed. With trembling hands she rummages through her prescriptions, finds the one she was looking for, pops the cap, and swallows two.

"Maybe you're taking too many pills," I whisper. I ball my hands into fists, anticipating a second attack. But she stays put.

She glares at me, her eyes steely yet empty. "Maybe you should stop stuffing your face when I'm not looking."

I wish I could punch something right now. I wish I could call my mother a bitch. I hate everything about everything.

It seems we are at an impasse—locked eyes and loaded words. Who will make the first move?

Me.

"All that crap you take"—I point to her nightstand— "makes you mean." My mother wasn't like this until my father left. She used to cut the crusts off my PB&Js and sing me to sleep and bake cookies and help me with my homework and smile. It's as if someone erased her and drew me a new mom who hides in her bedroom, gobbles pills, falls asleep at the dinner table, and cries a lot.

She just stares at me defiantly. Then she buries her face in her hands. Her body shakes as she gulps for air. It's hard to watch, but I'm not coming to her rescue with hugs and words of reassurance. Not after what she just said to me.

To avoid looking at her, I glance around her bedroom. Why have I never noticed how depressing it is? Labeled boxes of our old life line two walls, stacked floor to ceiling. GOOD CHINA, FAMILY RM KNICKKNACKS, CHRISTMAS DECORATIONS, SOFTBALL PICS & MOVIES. I feel a new whoosh of sadness. We have no use for the good china anymore; there's no one to entertain. Holidays are depressing. We have no family room. And my softball career is over.

The room is gaunt like my mother. There's a bed, a nightstand, a dresser, and that's it. No artwork. No photographs.

No decorations. My mother's bedroom is filled with misery.

"Aren't you going to ask me why I got fired?"

Even though I have a suspicion, I still bite. "Why did you get fired?"

"Because I screwed up. Happy?" She breaks eye contact. "I didn't think they'd notice. I only took a couple. I . . ." Her voice trails off.

I knew it. She stole pills. "Are they pressing charges?"

She shakes her head. "Not if I go to rehab." She collapses again into sobs.

Rehab? How the hell is she going to go to rehab and still take care of us? I refuse to live with my father and his dumbass bride. I'd take Meggie and go live in a homeless shelter before I'd shack up with those two assholes.

She gets ahold of herself. "Meggie?"

I nod that I'll go pick her up.

As I walk the two blocks to Mrs. McNash's I replay the scene. My mother is a prescription-drug addict who stole pills from the pharmacy and got fired for it. That's messed up. By the number of pill bottles on her nightstand, she's taking more than I know about. I wonder what she'd do if I dumped her pill collection into the toilet and flushed it.

I exhale loudly. She'd get more, that's what she'd do. The woman needs rehab. But I'm back to my original concern:

Who would take care of us? I mean, technically I take care of Meggie a lot already, so I could do it, but would I be allowed?

I ring the bell at Mrs. McNash's. There's a HELP WANTED sign taped next to the door.

"Oh, hello, Dell. Come on in," Mrs. McNash says. The woman is always smiling, and her happiness is real. I can tell. She greets me the same way every day—with kindness.

"Hi." I watch Mrs. McNash's helper chase one of the toddlers, laughing. Could I work here? I'm probably not qualified, but if I got the job, I could give the money to my mother.

"You okay?" she asks me, her head tilted with concern. I was probably making some dumb face.

"Yeah. Sorry. What's the job for?" I mumble.

"Come again?"

I repeat my question.

"It's a part-time job. . . ."

I try not to blink as she talks. Mrs. McNash sees me. Her eyes don't leave mine, and her smile is about as genuine as my sister's. I wonder if she's always seen me and I was just too preoccupied to notice.

I study her as she goes on and on about the position. I should probably be paying attention, but I can't. She's so soothing. Not like a gray-haired, shawl-wearing granny. She's too young for that. More like a slightly plump, cheerful, middle-aged, gentle-voiced angel. She reaches over and puts her hand on my shoulder. I let the deep warmth penetrate my skin, and I wish I could ask her for a hug. But that would be weird.

"Oh, honey, I didn't even think of you, because I know you have softball. And besides, you wouldn't want to be chasing these little rugrats around in these small rooms. It's pretty tight quarters."

My mouth droops. I get it. She doesn't want to hire me because I'm enormous. I'd probably trip and crush one of these kids. Then it'd be all over the news that I was a rapist baby-killer.

By the time Meggie is in my arms, I am officially *not* hired.

This Moment Is Officially Smeared

BACK AT THE APARTMENT, I POP A PEANUT BUTTER cookie in my mouth and chew as quietly as I can. I don't want my mother to emerge from her bedroom in a cloud of "What the hell are you eating now, Adele?" rage. I absentmindedly reach for another one and come up empty-handed. I've eaten the entire box. Every damn cookie is gone.

Day one of my diet is ruined.

I stare at the cookie crumbs. Cookies make me feel . . . I don't know how cookies make me feel. I press down on the crumbs, making them stick to my finger. Cookies make me feel un-hungry. I scrape the crumbs from my fingertip with my bottom teeth and think—*I guess I'll have to fess up about softball soon.* My mother probably won't give a damn about that. She'll hyperfocus on the money wasted on my special-order uniform.

I haven't told my mother about the talent show, either. Apparently I'm not telling my mother anything anymore. I don't think she's capable of producing any normal motherly reactions: concern, empathy, pride. And I can't handle her dead stare.

If my sister were older, I would talk to her. Meggie was so cute when I picked her up from day care. She said, "I miss you, Dehwy, when you go." Then she kissed me right on the lips. She tasted like strawberries. I held her the whole walk home and breathed her in. By the time we got back, I swear I felt better. I don't know what it is about her smell, but I'm pretty sure it's what heaven smells like.

I grab the cookie packaging, roll it up tight, fish the empty bag of chips from the bottom of the trash can, and tuck it inside. My mother will go ballistic if she finds out that I've polished off the chips *and* the cookies. She just bought them.

Mom hasn't emerged from her bedroom since we got home ten minutes ago.

I change Meggie's diaper and have a brainstorm. I know how I can get my mother some money. It comes to me all at once, like a lightning strike to the brain. I do a quick online search, pack five plastic grocery bags full of clothes, tell my mom I'm taking Meggie for a walk, and head out. I'm struggling to push my sister and control the overflowing basket underneath her stroller. One bag keeps falling out every time we hit a bump.

The basket is stuffed with my clothes. I'm going to sell the tagged clothes from my closet that are too small for me to the resale shop in town. The money will take some pressure off my mother. In my estimation, I have about eight hundred to a thousand bucks worth of new clothes. I'm figuring I can walk out with around two hundred dollars—maybe even more if the stars align.

As I walk, I stare down at my sister. Meggie loves me. The way her little face lights up when I pick her up at day care makes me happier than anything on this planet. She's the only person in my life who hasn't let me down yet.

A bell tinkles as I enter the consignment store. I immediately see that pushing this stroller around just won't work. The place is so full of clothing racks and shelves of shoes that I don't even see the little old woman who works there until she is right in front of me.

"Well, hello there, pretty girl," she singsongs. She's leaning over, talking directly to Meggie. Meggie's little hand reaches out and rubs the woman's wrinkly cheek. "Oh, aren't you just the sweetest little thing."

The woman stands up straight, and can't be any more than four feet tall. "How may I help you, young lady?" She has a beautiful smile, and I get lost in it—the way her eyes kind of disappear into the happiness and how her cheeks plump up. She's glowing.

"Dear? What can I do for you today?"

"I want to sell this stuff." I bend down, grab two of the bags, and the woman gets right to work. The whole thing takes about an hour, and Meggie is amazing; she reads and sings and plays with her shoelaces and is basically the best little kid ever born. The woman—Eleanor—explains that she's giving me twenty percent of what they'll sell the stuff for. I walk out of the consignment shop with $279 in cold hard cash. That will definitely help my mom with this month's rent.

I make a mental note to thank my grandmother the next time I see her. She lives in Colorado, so that probably won't be for a long time.

I'm actually kind of glad they never fit, because now I can hand my mother this nice hunk of cash.

Who knew my grandmother would show up out of the blue with bags of new clothes for me? Or that it would end up being profitable?

I remember that day so clearly. My mom and I didn't even know my grandmother was in town. I felt embarrassed because she bought everything in a size twelve. According to my grandmother, size twelve is a plus size, and the only other person who wears a size twelve is her friend Liz, who eats nonstop and can never get her pants buttoned even though they are a size twelve.

Needless to say, I'm no size twelve. I was a ten before my dad swallowed his Super-Dick serum, and that was two years ago. I think my grandmother meant well. I'm convinced her grand gesture was to try to make up for my father, her son, ruining our family. But I guess she figured anyone over a size twelve doesn't deserve clothes that fit.

Meggie says, "Yay, Dehwy. Birdies. Yook!"

I stop pushing her stroller and glance toward where she's pointing. There, up in the tree, are a cardinal and a blue jay sitting side-by-side on one of the lower branches. Chirping away to each other like two old friends catching up. I've never seen that before.

"I see, Megs, I see. Wow, girl!"

We watch the two birds. Their necks are turned, and they stare at each other more intensely than the human beings I know. These two birds see each other. Unbelievable.

I pick up my pace because the late-afternoon sky, with its shades of violet and orange, reminds me that Meggie needs dinner, and I haven't even started my homework. As I wait for the streetlight to change, I inhale the warm spring air, and the most bizarre fantasy unravels in my head: Brandon secretly likes me because I know how to make him laugh. My size doesn't matter to him, and he's broken up about what he did to me at the party, so he dumps bitchy Taryn because she bores him and only cares about herself. Then he asks me out.

I am completely aware that it is stupid and impossible. I guess it boils down to this—I liked Brandon a lot, and I wanted him to kiss me and touch me. Deep down I wanted to have sex with him. And I keep trying to alter what actually happened that night so it resembles one of my fantasies.

But nothing I do blocks out Brandon's demand that I stay still. That I said no. That he left me naked and alone. I swear every stupid flower in Melissa's parents' bedroom shook its head at me as I pulled my underwear back on. None of my excuses can forgive how he treated me in the hallway. That look he had on his face—that scowl. He called me "dude."

I grip the stroller handles. I didn't fight harder and push him off of me for three reasons:

1. Because he's hot.
2. Because he complimented my seventh-grade
   grand slam.

3. Because I don't think anyone else will want to have
   sex with me, and I didn't want to die a virgin.

And maybe because I was scared.

Meggie is down for the night, and I'm finishing up my homework at the kitchen table. My mother emerges from her bedroom like a shadow, mumbles something about meeting a friend for dinner, and leaves. I'll have to wait to present her with the money.

I head into the living room and turn on the TV. After two commercials for fast food make me hungry again, I turn it off and sit in silence for a while. I even try watching some magic videos on my phone, but quickly abandon that because I can't stand the people and their confused smiles.

I allow my head to fall back and stare at the ceiling. Everything is pretty messed up right now. After a few minutes, the quiet gets to me. I grab the remote to turn on some background noise. My head won't shut off, worrying about what school will be like tomorrow and how many people saw that cow drawing. The next thing I know, I'm walking into my mother's bedroom. The storage box labeled SOFTBALL PICS & MOVIES is in my grasp in no time. I close her door behind me and head back to the living room.

The box is heavy—full of me. I'm glad I only have two paces until I can put it down on the coffee table. I sit on the sofa and wring my hands. This box represents my life back when my father loved me. Skinny me. Happy me. The me with two parents who kissed me good night and kissed each other over scrambled eggs in the morning. Complete me. The me I liked.

I reach up and tuck my hair behind my ears. SOFTBALL PICS & MOVIES. How could my father have left all of this? He didn't take a single photo or movie with him. Not one physical memory of our years together accompanied him to his new life. It's all been sealed away in this box, like a mummy encased in cardboard and clear packing tape. I peel off the tape and remove the lid. A waft of musty paper hits my nose. It reminds me of when we used to decorate our house at Christmas and I'd rummage through the boxes, deciding what decorations my mother and I would hang up next. Stale odor or not, it still smells of living and happy.

I pull out a stack of photos. The first image is of eight-year-old me in my red-and-white softball uniform, both of my arms wrapped around my father's waist. I'm looking up at him, and he's looking down at me. We're both smiling. I'm missing a few teeth. I hold the photo closer to my face. He looks like he loves me. I turn it over. Printed neatly in my father's handwriting, it says: Softball Champs—Adele hit winning run.

Maybe my father loved my athletic ability, not me. How could a man love his child and then abandon her? That's not love. That's bullshit.

Seeing this photograph fuels my desire to understand my relationship with my father. I search through the box. I read the meticulously labeled DVD cases and grab the one I want: ADELE—FRESHMAN YEAR—AVERAGE PERFORMANCE. This was the last game that my father came to. Two weeks later, my family collapsed into chaos. Even though I've never seen this video, I'm confident it is going to prove my theory right.

I push the DVD in and press play. The first thing I hear are the birds. My father must not have known that the camera was on, because all I see is grass and, occasionally, the side of his sneaker. My mother's voice asks me if I have my water bottle. Still grass on the screen.

Then the shot goes haywire because my father is walking, but the sound is still crystal clear. "Adele, remember, if they move their fielders out toward the fence, hit a grounder. Don't mess up today. My boss is coming, 'kay?"

That bit of dialogue is an unexpected bonus. Dad definitely didn't know he was being taped. The screen switches to the field—he is holding the camera.

K. M. Walton

I watch the whole game, which doesn't take too long, since my father only videoed when I was up at bat. I struck out once, hit a fly ball to center field for the out, and got an RBI. Not a great game for me. Not my most memorable times at bat. But I remember every single second. I can still smell the fresh-cut grass and see the smoke rising from the neighbor's yard next to the field as he burned his grass clippings.

"Not your best game, Adele," I hear my father say. He is zoomed in on my face for reasons unknown.

"Sorry, Dad." I squint because the sun is in my eyes. Then I smile at the camera. My mother stands next to me. She has a little bulge in her sweatpants. That's unborn Meggie in there.

Mom asks the camera, "Lenny, is Mr. Thomas coming over for dinner?"

"No, I'm taking him out. I told you that already. Why do I bother talking?"

I study my face carefully to see if my parents' bickering affects me. I roll my eyes. I appear to be uncomfortable, nervous even, as they go back and forth a few more times about talking and listening. I press stop and lean back on the sofa.

Not once did my father hug me. There was no high five, no compliment. Just a single line of critique.

My theory is correct. My father didn't love me; he loved my athletic ability.

empty

My eyes dart around the room as I search my memory for more proof. I recall game after game that my father showed me love—but only when I played well.

I toss the DVD back in the box and slam the lid. This was a bad idea. Why am I torturing myself? I put the box away so my mother won't know that I was in her room, then plop back on the sofa. I wonder if my father would've left if Meggie had been a boy. I don't think he ever wanted me, either. This makes my lips quiver. How shallow and disgusting can one man be? How can this shallow and disgusting man be my father?

I stare at the wall for at least an hour and shift my weight because something is poking my butt through my jeans.

The wad of cash. I forgot about the money for my mother.

"Dell?" my mother calls. She's home now from wherever the hell she was. I really don't want to know the details. I'd like to sneak past her and disappear underneath my covers, but I have to give her this money.

I meet her in the kitchen. "I have something for you," I mumble under my breath.

She stops riffling through the mail and looks at me with a frown. "Speak clearly. Say it again."

"I said, I have something for you." I wish I had it in me to get all excited like Cara does. Smile. Squeal.

K. M. Walton

She raises her eyebrows. Her skin is pale. If she weren't standing there scowling at me, I'd think she was dead.

I hand her the cash.

"W-what's this?" she stutters.

"It's for you."

She squints. "Where did you get this?" She counts it. "This is a lot of money here. Where did this come from?" She sounds worried—angry, almost.

"It's all yours. That should help, right?"

She puts the money on the kitchen table and whispers, "Adele, where did that money come from?"

Wow, this is so not turning out how I envisioned it. I imagined my mother hugging me and tears and some oh-you-are-the-best-daughter-a-mom-could-ever-have shit. Not scowls and suspicion. I can't win.

"Mom, seriously, calm down. I didn't steal it or anything. I . . ." I go quiet because I don't want to tell her I sold the clothes. They're the same clothes she pesters me to wear every day.

"You what?" she prompts.

I blurt out, "I sold my clothes."

My mother pounds the counter and throws the mail at me.

I duck and yell, "Oh my God, Mom. You're acting like I sold crack or gave hand jobs on the corner. What the hell?"

"Hand jobs? What are you talking about?" she yells back.

The moment is officially ruined, so I blabber out the whole story all at once. "I felt bad about last night and how much money Daddy owes you. I thought I could sell the clothes in my closet to help out with bills. So that's what I did. I sold my clothes. They didn't fit anyway. There, are you happy now? I'm not some drug-dealing whore. Does that make you happy, Mom? Because all I wanted to do was make you happy."

I can't hold back my tears, and this aggravates me. I hate when I'm the only one crying. This makes me fume even more. Before I can stop myself, I punch the wall next to the refrigerator. It makes an indent in the drywall.

"Adele! Stop it! Stopitstopitstopitstopit!" my mother screeches.

"Why is this MY life?" I scream at the top of my lungs. Then I run the five measly steps to the bathroom and slam the door so hard that my towel, which had been hanging on the hook, falls to the ground. I kick it. It is completely unsatisfying, which makes me want to punch something again. I slam down the toilet lid and sit. After rocking back and forth a few times, I realize that I can't stay in here all night. I need to let the rage out.

I fling open the bathroom door, ready to stomp across the hall, when I hear Meggie whimpering in our room.

"Damnit." I cringe and turn my head, fully expecting my

mother to come flying down the hallway, furious that I've woken Meggie up.

She doesn't.

I wait a few minutes to see if she will fall back to sleep on her own. My hand hurts from punching the wall. I rub it as anger bashes my insides—my heart, my brain.

I can't stand here another second. I need to do something.

I tiptoe into my room and slide into my bed. I want to kick my feet and curse and go completely nuts, but I can't. Meggie's settled herself, and I don't want to wake her again, so I clutch my pillow and silently scream into it. I press my face down into my pillow, deeper, deeper, deeper.

My mother doesn't come to apologize or comfort me, and I guess I fall asleep, because when I open my eyes it's pitch-black. My first thought? How could she not have checked on me? How could she let me melt down alone? Doesn't she care how I feel? My answer is: no.

My mother is a zombie. Her heart is dead. Her soul is withered.

My alarm clock says it's 2:46. I sit up and blink a few times. My stomach growls, and my eyes hurt. My eyelids feel like I put Novocain in them. You know, like when you come from the dentist and your lips feel like you shoved a football underneath the skin? That's how my eyes feel.

I walk down to the bathroom. My skin is red and blotchy, and my eyes are swollen to slits. I splash cold water on my face and let it run down my neck. I'm hoping it'll wake me up. My whole body feels numb. I puff my cheeks with air a few times and check the mirror to see if I look more alive. I look the same. I brush my teeth and pee.

I check my reflection again, and it's just as awful.

The next day in English class, I'm focused on getting my stuff organized on my desk and ignoring that Sydney's behind me. Mrs. Salvatore has her back to us, writing discussion questions on the whiteboard. The sound of her squeaking marker blends with that of student voices. We're allowed to talk to each other, but only until she stops writing and starts class with her usual "Game on, people, game on." Then we all have to shut up.

Sydney taps me on the shoulder.

I just turn my head. "Hey." I don't want to talk to her, be interrogated by her, or have her tell me things I'm not supposed to know—like how Taryn's got the hots for Jacob. I look back up front.

She taps me again.

"Dell?" She sounds nervous.

I swivel in my seat this time.

Her eyes drop, and she leans forward, her hair touching

K. M. Walton

the desk. I'm waiting for her to start talking, but her face twists into a weird frowny wince.

"Are you all right?" I ask. She looks constipated.

"I have to tell you something," she whispers through clenched teeth.

Right away, two thoughts cross my mind:

1. Sydney told Taryn that I went upstairs with Brandon at Melissa's party, and they both assume that I had sex with Brandon.
2. Sydney drew the cow and taped it to my locker.

"Game on, people, game on!" Mrs. Salvatore announces from the front.

"Forget it," Sydney says. "Never mind."

As my heart slows down a little, I raise my eyebrows and shrug. Sydney closes her eyes. She is acting so bizarre. I face front and leave her to her thoughts.

Running

I WANT A LOT OF THINGS I CAN NEVER HAVE: A different body, my virginity back, for Brandon and whoever taped that drawing to my locker to explode like watermelons stuffed with dynamite, a best friend who would die for me, way less math homework, and cute clothes to wear for the talent show on Friday.

At yesterday's rehearsal, I decided I'm lucky to have a friend, and let Cara talk me into sticking with the talent show. Now I am sitting in the cafeteria, pushing dressing-soaked salad around on my tray. I'm back on a diet and gave myself a verbal lashing in the mirror this morning before school. I really let myself have it for eating those cookies and chips.

Cara says, "You have to smile at the end, Dell. You looked scared up there yesterday. Just smile, and it'll make the audience think you're a pro."

"I'm not a pro, Cara. What's the opposite of pro?"

"Amateur."

"I'm below an amateur."

She rolls her eyes. "That's what I'm talking about. You don't have to let the audience know that. Will you listen to me for once? What are you wearing? You haven't said a word." She grimaces. "I'm worried."

With my fork, I roll a cherry tomato from one side of the tray to the other. "You're worried? Way to have faith in me." I shove a bite of lettuce into my mouth so that I don't have to say anything else.

"You're avoiding the question! You are not wearing jeans, are you? Look me in the eye and tell me you have something to wear tomorrow night. Don't embarrass us."

Embarrass us? *So now she's embarrassed by me?*

I swallow. "Will you shut up? I've got it under control." Which is about as far from the truth as I am skinny. I have nothing to wear. I have nothing planned. I have zero under control.

I won't tell Cara this. Her eyeballs will pop from their sockets and bounce around the cafeteria if she knows. She needs her eyes to play the piano. I spare her my clothing dilemma by keeping my mouth shut. She's practically growling at me from across the table anyway, so I give her the I'm-just-scratching-my-temple middle finger.

Salad churns in my stomach. My wounded feelings twist and tangle around my neck, nearly strangling the life out of me. I cough into my napkin and quietly fight for a new breath.

Cara grins and deadpans, "You're so funny." She's clearly oblivious to my desperation. She's *just scratching her temple* too. "Smile during today's practice, and fuck you, too."

I manage to inhale *and* keep the salad down, which is a miracle, but I think I'd rather have just passed out. Lifeless and facedown in my tray.

After talent show rehearsal, Cara and I are talking in the hall and about to head home, when Emma shows up. She looks directly at Cara. "Did you hear about her?" She tilts her head toward me.

"I know, Em, Dell was un-freaking-believable up there!" Cara's voice shines with enthusiasm. "I am so proud of her."

Emma shakes her head. "No, not that." She turns and walks away, then shouts over her shoulder, "Forget it. I can't say it with her, like, right there and staring at me like that. Taryn messaged us on Facebook."

I immediately pull out my phone and log on. Cara gasps, obviously beating me to the punch. I look from my phone to her face. I don't see what she's freaking out about.

"You're not . . ." Cara's voice trails off as her face tightens with confusion. "You're not in the message group, Dell."

Panicked, I blurt, "What is it? What does it say?"

She doesn't answer me. I move so I can read over her shoulder.

Taryn: You guys!!!!! Dell the fat whore raped my boyfriend.

Chase: dude, she screwed B-man? ew, i just puked in my
     mouth.

Melissa: WHAT?!?!

Taryn: He was drunk and she pinned him down at your
     party. Sydney said she saw them go upstairs. She told
     me so yesterday. Brandon admitted it just now. He said
     she almost killed him, the fat pig.

Emma: I'm not surprised!

Taryn: Beware of the rapist bovine, Cara. I heard she ate
     her best friend in kindergarten.

This is all wrong. All wrong. All wrong. I drift a few feet away from Cara and the wrongness.

"Wh-what," she stammers and clears her throat. "What is this about?"

I turn around. Cara's eyes flutter and blink—it's like she can't even look at me.

Despite my frozen stance, my brain is on overload.

This can't be real.

He can't be that much of an asshole.

He complimented my grand slam, and he was sincere.

He led me upstairs with his grins and his flirting.

He raped *me*.

I have to tell the truth.

I can't tell the truth.

This is all wrong.

He raped *me*.

But who would believe me? Who would believe that he came on to me, that it was his idea to go upstairs, that he held me down and had sex with me? I couldn't handle watching people wince with doubt. The eye rolls. The probing questions. Continuously having to validate the truth. That would feel as invasive and humiliating as the rape itself.

I've wrecked my friendship with Cara by not telling her right after it happened. Cara will never trust me again. She will hate me.

"I don't—" My teeth chatter in my mouth. I've suddenly turned cold. "I can't—"

"God, Dell, what are you saying?" Cara says. "Is this true?"

The JV cheerleading team jogs past the auditorium, laughing noisily. I don't answer Cara. I want silence. I want to hide.

Brandon's little sister stops in front of us, and I watch Cara's face light up. She's insta-happy.

Cara says, "Hi, Kim!" *Cara knows her first name?*

Kim blows her a kiss. "Bye, Cara, gotta go," she says in her best cheer voice. Kim's black ponytail bobs as she jogs to catch up with the rest of her team.

Cara turns back to me. Gone are the bright eyes and blinding smile. She's back to grimace-face. "We just broke in! How could you do that? Taryn is a bitch. You do know she'll ruin you, right?"

Why isn't she asking me what really happened?

I am stunned by Cara's ability to turn her popular-girl greeting on and off so quickly.

Cara yanks my arm. "Everything's ruined now."

I break her grip and run.

A Damn Mess

I RUN ALL THE WAY HOME, WHICH IS A MIRACLE, considering how much I hate running. After composing myself in the bathroom, I creep to the kitchen as quietly as I can. My mother is locked in her bedroom again. I sit at the table with the very un-diet and very empty "family size" bag of cheese puffs. I'm staring at the dent I made in the wall, when my phone buzzes again. I have a bunch of missed calls from Cara and four texts in a row that each say:

SORRY!

I don't answer. The phone vibrates and I know she's left a message. I listen: *Dell, I suck. I'm sorry I reacted that way. We need to talk!*

That is the deepest Cara's ever been with me in our seven-year friendship.

She should be sorry.

My mother shuffles into the kitchen. "Hey." She eyes the empty bag.

I wish I'd thrown it away after I'd finished eating, but it's too late now. "Hey." I sit up a little bit. Maybe the empty bag won't matter. Maybe she wants to apologize for how she reacted when I gave her the money.

She walks to the sink and starts washing dirty dishes. "I can't afford your appetite, Adele. Look, I'm in a bad way. You have to understand where I'm coming from."

Some apology. She acts like I purposefully eat to make things harder on her. Doesn't she know that we're both messed up? She pops pills and I eat cheese puffs. She acts like I wasn't affected when Dad left. My world sucked too, but she acts like I don't understand anything.

Shit, I wonder if she found out about my father getting remarried. I can't believe I have to deal with all of this. Anger begins to bubble up from inside. I do not want to explode again. I grasp the sides of my chair and swallow my resentment. I just let her keep talking.

"You eat too much, and you're unhealthy. There, I said it."
She exhales loudly.

I want to say, "No shit, Sherlock, and you're the pill-popping walking dead." I stare at the empty cheese-puff bag instead. There are orange crumbs all over the table. It's a mess.

I'm a mess.

She's a mess.

My whole life is a damn mess.

All I want to do is lick the salty cheese off the inside of the bag.

Mom wipes her hands on her FoodMart shirt. "I can't believe he's marrying her. I don't know why I wasn't good enough for him. We had a life."

So she does know. He must have told her. I stay quiet and let my mother have this moment of introspection. I can't imagine losing everything simply because my husband stopped loving me.

I squint.

Wait a second. That's not true. I *can* imagine it, because that same man stopped loving me, and I lost everything too. Even my identity. I've eaten the girl I was before, swallowed her down with cookies and ice cream and cheese puffs.

My mother and I lock eyes.

"I guess I freaked out about the money because you and

Meggie are all I've got left, and I want you to make smart decisions."

I guess we're off the topic of my overeating. I go with it. "Are you saying that giving you two hundred seventy-nine dollars to help pay the rent was a bad decision?"

"No." She stares into the living room introspectively. "I don't know what I'm saying. My whole damn life has been turned upside down."

I want to ask my mom what pills she stole from the drugstore. I want to ask her to dump every bottle in the toilet and flush it all away. Did she look into rehab yet so we can all start over? "So you don't want the money?"

"No, I—"

I cut her off and yell, "I can't believe you!" Then I bring it down a bit. "I can't believe you aren't thanking me and telling me that I am the best daughter in the world. What the hell, Mom?"

She presses her lips together. "You didn't let me finish. I will take the money. Thank you."

That seemed hard for her to say. Is it pride?

I shrug.

Then mom says quietly, "Were you going to tell me about softball?"

How did she find out? Did Coach call her? Why would Coach do that? Or maybe it was my stupid father.

I don't want to fight with my mother, so I stay silent. She starts chewing her nail. Her hand is shaking. I've never seen her bite her nails before.

"Don't give me the silent treatment."

This startles me, and my knee hits the table leg, knocking over the salt and pepper shakers. The salt rolls off the table and across the floor, stopping at my mother's feet. She bends over and grabs it in a flash. She looks like she's going to throw it at me. I cover my face for protection.

"I'm not going to throw it at you," she says, her voice expressionless.

I bring my arms back to my sides. I'm tired of talking. I want to go to my room.

"I need you to pick up Meggie," my mother says. "I have the night shift. I've gotta be out of here in twenty."

I wish my mother was a hugger. A hug right now would help a lot. A hug would fill me up, make me feel as if I exist, and maybe even douse the anger. Instead I get a shoulder squeeze as my mom heads back to her room. A shoulder squeeze can in no way be compared to a hug. They're like the difference between a size twenty-four and a size two. The squeeze is so inadequate, and the hug just the right thing.

I want perfect and I get insufficient.

• • •

K. M. Walton

Meggie pounds on her high-chair tray because she wants more macaroni and cheese. I stare down at my raw carrots, push my plate away, and start to cry. I'm starving. I'm fat. The carrots were my third attempt at dieting—after the bag of cheese puffs—and I'm sick of dieting. It's been exactly one hour, and I'm a failure.

I am a phony, rapist failure.

I give my sister more mac and cheese, then grab a spoon to eat it straight out of the pot. Each bite of gooey, cheesy noodles explodes in my mouth with flavor. My heart stops racing, and I feel a distinct sense of pleasure each time I swallow. Those carrots can suck it. So can everyone at school.

I'm mortified by what Taryn and Chase said on Facebook. The way they bantered back and forth, all "ha-ha, she's a fat rapist, ha-ha," was evil. How can I possibly face them in school? They've probably told the entire world by now.

Sydney is a bitch. She doesn't even know the truth. She fabricated and assumed and blabbed her stupid mouth and now everything's even worse.

To calm myself down, I make a fresh batch of mac and cheese and eat every noodle. The buttery cheese clouds my head, helping me to forget the hideous Facebook comments. As I'm scraping out the last bits of orange from the pot, I pause. *You promised yourself you would stick with the diet.* How will I ever look normal if I eat two boxes of macaroni and cheese for dinner? The answer comes quickly, like a smack to the forehead: I won't.

Taunts and insults continue to torture me as I get the dishes cleaned up—even as I bathe Meggie and tuck her into her crib. In spite of the mental torment, I manage to tackle my math homework and a box of cherry frosted Pop-Tarts. Pink frosted crumbs fall on my notebook and into the spine of my textbook. I slam both books shut and rehash everything again.

And I gag.

I force myself to swallow the Pop-Tart that's in my mouth. I don't feel like cleaning up puke right now. I drop my head into my hands. My reality assaults me. That whole group thinks I held Brandon down at the party and raped him, like a disgusting pig. I don't even know what Cara believes, and that hurts.

It all hurts, and I'm so tired of feeling alone.

I can't sleep. My brain runs through a thousand scenarios about how I could get out of school. Permanently. Then, around three thirty in the morning, I decide that I will do what I always do: fake it. But instead of making people like me because I make them laugh, I will drop my eyes and act like I don't exist. I won't listen to what they say. I'll ignore them, and hopefully, they will ignore me.

I just don't want to deal with the stares, mean comments, and whispers. I want someone else to do something stupid, so everyone can move on to the next bullshit drama. But I don't know if I'll ever be able to move on. I feel stained, like, ruined.

At least Taryn's comment was in a private message group and not out there for all of Facebook to see. I think I will die if any of this leaks out to my teachers or counselors. Discussing those evil comments—or what actually happened that night—with an adult would be as awful as being naked onstage. And in the meantime, I will be praying on my knees that some mutant parasite embeds itself into the balls of Brandon Levitt, eating him alive from the inside out.

That would help me through this day.

I break into a light sweat as I cross the back field. Cara's up ahead, sitting on the wall. She's alone. Thank God.

"Hey," I say to Cara. She's zoned out with her headphones in, so I wave my hand in front of her face to get her attention. She jumps.

She pulls out her earbuds. "Hey."

I scrunch my nose. "I got your texts and your voice mail."

"I tried to get Taryn to delete those comments, but . . ." Her voice trails off.

I know Cara can't control other people and what they put on the Internet. There are probably even more comments now. "Thanks." I can't tell if she believes me or Taryn, and I'm afraid to ask. I'm worried she'll think Brandon's side of the story is true. I can't be friends with Cara if she thinks I raped him, and she's all I've got. I have to tell her the truth.

"Cara, I should've—"

Cara's face tightens, and I stop. Taryn's laugh comes from behind me. I squeeze my eyes shut for a second. I wish I could run home and lock myself in my bedroom with a trunk of food and water and never come out.

I turn, half expecting Taryn to be right behind me with a samurai sword or some other glamorous weapon, poised to dismember me right there on the sidewalk. She's with that gaggle of freshman cheerleaders I saw at the movies. Taryn's face lights up as they all flit around her like bugs to the zapper. It's clear she loves the attention.

Popularity is a strange thing. I mean, Taryn wouldn't acknowledge the existence of those girls, let alone speak to them, if they were ugly or overweight. But since they're "popular" and all have matching ponytails and cute little bodies, she's over there holding court. I watch as she fixes one girl's ribbon and puts lip gloss on Brandon's sister. Such sweet gestures.

Taryn says something, and the whole group whips around

to stare at me. They detonate into fits of laughter. Kim's not laughing, though; she's shaking her head back and forth, over and over again.

My ears fill with static, like someone shoved live wires in there. I turn my back on them. The white noise gets louder and louder. I swear my head might begin to spark and smoke. I need to sit down. I reach for the wall and somehow get all of me on it. I lean forward on my thighs and concentrate on not fainting. Where did Cara go?

Taryn's voice is very close now. "Brandon's sister, Kim, said he should press charges against you, Dell."

I open my eyes and lift my head to face Taryn. Her crew is set up behind her like bowling pins, with her as lead pin. If only I could roll a boulder into them, scattering their bodies all over the sidewalk. I stick to my plan and ignore Taryn's remark.

"Brandon told me he feels sorry for you, but I don't. Girls like you are dangerous when they're hungry."

Emma and Melissa snicker. Sydney plays with a loose strap on her backpack.

A burning sensation starts in my stomach. I see Cara now, but she's standing with her head down, and I swear it looks like she's one of the bowling pins. I look down at the sidewalk so I can think.

"Stop, Taryn."

They all turn to stare at Cara. "Just leave her alone," she whispers.

I want to scoop her into a bear hug.

"She was drunk." Cara crosses her arms. "She didn't know what she was doing."

I want to punch her in the face.

Taryn takes a step closer to Cara and leans in. "Whose side are you on, Cara? She raped my boyfriend!"

Why can't I tell them that Brandon forced himself on me? Took advantage of my drunkness, told me to stay still, and put himself inside me. I told him to stop. I didn't want to do it. Or did I? Oh my God, maybe I did. I'm, like, double his weight. I could've pushed him off me. Could I have? Maybe this *is* all my fault.

Taryn says, "I guess I don't have to worry about you coming after him again, bitch." Her voice lifts and fades. "Because I swear to God you look like you're about to explode. With. Just. One. More. Bite. Of. Food."

She pauses in between each word to emphasize her point. To be sure they cut me to the bone. My eyes decide to blink uncontrollably.

"Even if you lost weight you'd still look like an ugly man." Taryn turns on her heels, and all of her girls follow her—all but one. Cara.

"I told you she'd attack." Cara gathers her backpack. "You should've told me; that way I could've done damage control. Why didn't you tell me?"

I can't speak.

"Hello? Are you listening?"

Instead of answering her, I walk away.

Cara falls in stride with me. "It's just so unlike you to be aggressive with a guy. How many beers did you have?"

Her question shreds me to the core. I block Cara out. She hasn't once asked for my side of the story or even questioned the validity of Brandon's accusation. It sickens me to think that everyone just believes Brandon because he's popular and handsome. There is no justice for fat girls.

How am I going to make it through the entire school day? Facing class after class of people who, no doubt, will have heard Taryn's lies? And believed them?

"You know what, Dell?" Cara shouts, startling me. "I'm done with you ignoring me." I glare at her. She shakes her head. "And you can find your own way to the talent show tonight!" She stomps off, and I stand like a block of melting ice. The hallway is full of students scurrying around me.

The talent show—I'm not doing it.

Chase and Jacob and a bunch of other baseball guys come barreling down the hall, mooing and laughing and pointing at me. The warning bell rings, and they disperse before they reach me. I unfreeze and stagger a bit as I head toward my locker. I can't do this. I can't. I wipe the sweat from my forehead. Maybe I have a fever. I'll tell the nurse I threw up at home and puked in the bathroom here—which is something I think may actually happen.

I guess being called an ugly man by Taryn Anderson and the threat of being formally charged as a rapist can cause one's body temperature to rise, because I have a fever of 99.1. It's enough to get me a private cot in the nurse's office.

I'm curled up in the fetal position underneath a scratchy wool blanket, worrying if Brandon will press charges against me. It would be my word against his. How could I prove that I was the victim? I never reported it. Hell, I haven't told a single soul. Would the police believe me? If they're anything like the shits at my high school, I would be in serious trouble. I rock my body back and forth at the thought of having to go to jail.

There's a knock at the door, and the nurse peeks her head in. "You're awake. Good. Let me feel your head." She rests her open palm on my forehead, and it's freezing. I startle. "Sorry, sorry. My hands are always cold. Well, you still feel warm to me. It's fourth period now. If you want to go home, I'll have to call a parent."

I tell the nurse not to bother calling my mother, because she can't leave work, and ask her if I could just stay here.

"Let's give it another period and see how you feel. I'll be back with something to help settle your stomach."

The nurse cracks open my door, holding a package of crackers and a can of ginger ale. I am free to rest in here until I feel up to heading back to class.

I gag for effect as I reach for the food. She says, "I'll lay them over here for later." If she only knew how stressed out I am right now, and how I eat when anxious. She'd be relieved I didn't filet her and eat her.

Magic Isn't Real

A KNOCK WAKES ME UP. I STRETCH AND LOOK around. Oh yeah, I'm in the nurse's office. The details tumble from my head: the Facebook shit, Taryn's attack, Cara's abandoning me. Good times.

The nurse peeks her head in. "Hon, the last bell rang ten minutes ago. I let you sleep."

"Oh, thanks." I sit up and run my fingers through my matted hair. She walks over and feels my forehead again.

"How do you feel?"

Like a humiliated piece of shit. "Okay."

"Someone's here to see you."

My stomach tightens.

The nurse opens the door all the way, and I see that "someone" is the guidance counselor, Mr. Drueller. If Mr. Drueller's here, that means someone told him what's going on. That means he knows about the rape lie. The thought of discussing, addressing, mentioning, or referencing what Brandon did to me with Mr. Drueller—who is, like, ninety years old—makes me nauseous. I seriously might throw up. I'm dying inside.

"Adele, is there anything you'd like to talk about?" He takes one step into the small room.

Fuck no is what I'd like to respond. My mouth goes completely dry. I shake my head.

His forehead pinches. "Are you sure?"

Hell yeah, I'm sure.

We do that uncomfortable dance as we look at each other while trying to avoid eye contact.

"Okay, well, one of your peers is concerned about you and came to me. I am not at liberty to share who, but they said you may need to talk to an adult. That's all of the information that I could get out of the person. You know where my office is if you change your mind. It's my job to listen. I'm a pretty decent listener, and . . ." His voice trails off and he shoves his hands into his dress pants. He looks about as uncomfortable as I feel. I stare at the floor. "Okay, well, feel better," he says. The door clicks closed behind him, and I resume breathing.

Cara must have gone to see Mr. Drueller. Deep down this makes me want to forgive her. Again.

The nurse sets me free. As I walk, I clasp my hands together until my knuckles turn white. There are sure to be students in the building, and I don't want to see any of them. Not even for a split second.

I'm doing everything in my power to slink to my locker. A 286-pound girl is about as stealth as a rhino falling down the stairs. As I turn the corner there's a commotion up ahead. I come to a halt. What's going on at the end of the hallway could easily be classified as my worst nightmare.

Brandon and the baseball team are suited up and getting a pep talk from Coach Lein. I'm going to have to walk by them to get to my locker. Maybe if I stop and wait, they'll head out to the field, and I can escape unscathed. I get a very long drink from the water fountain. They shout their "Go Chargers" chant, and I watch them all start grabbing their stuff. Coach Lein heads out the door.

Chase sees me and shouts, "Moooo!" His tone is different this time, stripped of his usual lightheartedness. This moo sounds evil.

Brandon stands silently, glaring at me.

I want to grow wings and take flight. I want disappearing dust sprinkled on me. I want a wand waved, a lamp rubbed, heels clicked—anything to make me invisible right now. But I'm just your garden-variety fat girl, standing in her high school hallway. Magic isn't real.

Pain is real.

It's weird, this everyone-is-staring-at-everyone moment. My eyes dart from Brandon to Chase, back to Brandon. No one says a word. Then the spell breaks and everyone but Brandon turns their back on me and walks through the doors.

I'm alone in the hallway with Brandon. "Stay away from me, Dell!" He heads out into the sunshine.

My backpack feels weighted with bricks. I let it slide to the ground. I want to kick it. I want it to rocket through the doors and hit Brandon in the back, knocking the wind out of him. I want him to feel like I feel. Desperate for air.

My leg winds up and I unleash on my backpack. Upon impact, two things are immediately evident:

1. I have a wicked kick, because my backpack—
filled with two textbooks, two notebooks, and a binder—has taken quite a ride down the waxed school floor.
2. I have broken my big toe.

empty

I heard it crack. Like a stick snapping in half.

Halfway home I decide to pick up Meggie early. I am in excruciating pain, and the thought of having to navigate the stairs to my apartment twice is horrendous.

The rest of my walk to Mrs. McNash's is such a struggle. I try walking on my heel and hobbling on the outside of my foot to lessen the pain—nothing works. I know I can't tell my mother what I've done. She'll think it's ridiculous and blame my clumsiness on my weight, and then we'll wind up getting angry at each other. Each step, regardless of where my foot makes impact with the ground, hurts like hell.

Mrs. McNash is pretty perceptive, because she notices something's wrong the second she opens the door. "Adele, what's the matter, honey? Why are you making that face?"

I swallow. Maybe I should tell *her* what happened. Unload every heavy detail onto her warm, kind shoulders. Maybe she'd listen to me. . . . Maybe she'd believe me.

"Nothing," I say. "I tripped on the sidewalk. Stubbed my toe. I'm good."

Confusion registers on her face. "I don't know about that. Want me to take a look? It might be broken."

"Nah, really, I'm all right. It feels better already. I'll ice it when I get home."

Total lie.

K. M. Walton

I'm doing everything in my power not to cry in front of the woman. I blink a bunch of times and bite the inside of my lip.

"Oh, honey, you're as white as a ghost. Come here." She wraps me in a hug. I am hushed by the perfection of the embrace. The way her arms put just the right amount of pressure on my body makes me know that I exist. She smells like dryer sheets. She draws back but holds on to my shoulders. "Let me have one of my girls drive you and Meggie home."

I nod. I don't want her to let me go. Her touch is gentle and kind, and I haven't been touched like that in a long time. She probably thinks I'm a clingy weirdo, so I let my eyes wander past Mrs. McNash, into her living room. I spot Meggie. She's sleeping on her mat, butt up. Her blanket is tucked underneath her cheek. She's an angel.

"Let me get Meggie for you." Mrs. McNash skillfully steps over three kids, picks her up, and has Meggie in my arms without her making a peep.

"Dehwy!" she whispers in her groggy little voice. I gently smother her neck with kisses so Mrs. McNash can't see my tears. Her smell fills my nose, and I try to visualize Meggie's smell surrounding my body like a fog of perfection and innocence. Wrapping me in love.

I put Meggie down and change my mind about the ride.

"I can walk, really. Thanks though." I shift my weight and gasp. Not healed. I want the love to heal my broken bone. Still broken.

Mrs. McNash insists, so we get a ride home from Miss Kelly, the skinny twentysomething with superwhite teeth and neon orange hair who got the part-time job instead of me. The drive home is less than five minutes, but Miss Kelly manages to tell me that she went to my high school, got accepted to West Chester University for early childhood ed, hated studying, flunked out, and got the job with Mrs. McNash because she agreed to take classes at the community college, which she's not studying for either.

Fascinating.

I pant through my thank-you and hobble to the front landing with Meggie, her stroller, and my backpack in tow. Miss Kelly makes no move to help me. She's too busy texting up a storm. She honks as she drives away. There is no way in hell I will make it up the stairs while carrying everything, so I leave Meggie's folded stroller behind the main door.

The walk up the stairs is torture. I have to peel my fingers from the banister when Meggie and I reach the top. My teeth are probably nubs from all of my clenching and gritting. The f-word slips out as I unlock our door.

Meggie bounces into our apartment. "Fuck. Fuck. Fuck."

I shout to her as I close the door behind me, "Megs, that's not a nice word. You can't say that word. Okay?"

She scrunches her face into the cutest scowl. I get her set up with a snack and a video while I gobble ibuprofen. When I wrestle my foot out of my sneaker I almost puke. It's black and blue and swollen to twice its normal size. After a quick Internet search I learn that I have to stabilize my mangled toe. We don't have the right kind of tape, so I use regular, clear wrapping-paper tape. After much panting and sweating, I have squished my broken big toe and the one next to it together into one painful mess.

I lie down on the sofa and put a pillow underneath my foot to elevate it. Meggie is engrossed watching colorful little creatures dance and sing about friendship. I close my eyes, take deep breaths, and try not to pass out from the rolling waves of agony. The underlying hum of the traffic passing by calms me down.

My cell beeps, startling me, and I listen to a rambling voice mail from Cara. "I hope you're not going to weasel out of the talent show and stay home sulking, Dell. It was just sex—even if it was with the most popular girl's boyfriend. It was just sex. Besides, you can't hide out forever. Meet me at six, backstage by the lion head. Wear makeup, like, a lot. It's called stage makeup, and you need to make it dark or it won't show out in the audience."

I sit up because I can't believe what I just heard. Just sex? She still believes Brandon's story. I'm in the middle of texting Cara something along the lines of "Wow, you're lucky you told the guidance counselor you were worried about me, because if you hadn't, I'd be really mad at you right now" when my toe explodes with pain. I let out a long moan. I abandon the text and limp to the medicine cabinet to inspect prescription bottles. I know what I'm looking for. Vicodin. That oughta take the edge off. "Yessss," I hiss. I pop two and head back to elevate my toe and finish my text.

There is a lot of me to get situated, so it takes a while, and by the time I'm comfortable, I lose the desire to text Cara. She obviously doesn't get it.

After twenty minutes of robotically staring at the television, I feel the Vicodin kick in. When I blink, it's like my inner windshield wipers are turned on slow, because my eyes take a while to open. My heartbeat isn't racing anymore either. Everything has slowed down. But my toe still hurts like a mother.

My cell buzzes with a new text from Cara. She demands I get over the whole Taryn incident by blowing everyone's mind onstage tonight. She says it will show everyone that I've moved on. Then she reminds me about my makeup again.

I put my phone down. I blink, and my eyelids are in no hurry to open. If I took another Vicodin, I probably wouldn't care about being up onstage. Hell, with that much Vicodin in me, I probably wouldn't care if I were naked onstage. Doing jumping jacks.

A Demented Circus Clown

I IMAGINE THE HOT STAGE LIGHTS WARMING MY skin, my voice filling the auditorium. The audience loving me, clapping and chanting my name. Mountains of love and adoration directed at me. That sounds so good right now.

I want that.

A landslide of objections form. I have nothing to wear. I have a broken toe. How am I supposed to get to school? I can't walk. What if the baseball dicks show up and start mooing in the audience? What if Taryn is there? That would get ugly.

It seems like the universe or God or whatever is trying to give me signs. Don't do it, Adele. Just stay home and eat a sandwich. Stay away from that stage. Stay away from those people. Stay away from that moment.

That moment.

But I love that moment.

The rehearsals have been dipped in perfection. The applause and cheering. My stomach flipping with joy. The skin around my mouth tingling as my face burst into a smile. I want to feel that again. It made me feel seen—really seen. And alive. Even Mrs. Salvatore cheered.

I need to feel joy, especially after all the crap I went through at school today. It might fill some of the empty space inside of me.

I text Cara and ask her if she can pick me up because I hurt my toe on my walk home (lie) and don't feel like walking (truth). She texts back that I'm a klutz and she'll honk at quarter of six.

I guess I'm actually going to sing.

I look at my watch. I've got an hour and a half until my mother gets home. I didn't tell my parents about the show because they wouldn't care. My father is too busy gallivanting around with Donna anyway. But if I'm going to sing, then I need to shower so I'm ready to go as soon as Cara honks.

Meggie is mesmerized by her show. I hop to the bathroom. I've never been more thankful that we live in a tiny apartment. As the hot water pours down my body, the wrapping slides off my toes. I stare down at the wet mound of tape. "Mother-effer."

After my shower I hop back to the kitchen to rewrap my toes. More swearing and more pain.

Four hops to my bedroom with freshly wrapped toes, and I'm searching for my black T-shirt with the white tree on it. It's my nicest one, and doesn't everyone say black makes you look skinnier? It takes me almost five minutes to get my jeans on because of my stupid toe. Even sliding the worn cotton over my toe makes me gag into my bent elbow. Those two Vicodin aren't touching the pain. I take a third. I figure that should take the edge off the throbbing and give me a nice buzz.

I stand in front of the bathroom mirror, caking on my mother's eye shadow. I have no clue how to put this on. Painting my droopy eyelids with a shaky hand isn't easy. I am awful at applying makeup. That third Vicodin must be kicking in, because I'm having trouble keeping my eyes open. I rub my cheeks to blend in my blush, and my skin feels like warm pudding. I need to sit down. My chin drops to my chest, and my body slowly tips to the right. I reach out and fumble for the towel bar. I steady myself.

"Whoa." I'm feeling pretty wasted right now.

A laugh builds in my chest, then bursts from my mouth.

K. M. Walton

I spray spit all over my reflection in the mirror and yell out, "Ugly!" I need more makeup. Cara said so.

This time I don't bother looking at the colors as I apply. My hand just swipes and smears over and over and over again. It has to be dark enough now. I squint and concentrate. My makeup can't get any darker. I bet when I'm onstage, I'll be visible from the baseball field across campus. This makeup can power through walls. Lockers. Solid brick. It's that heavy.

"Girls," my mother shouts. "I'm home!"

I have no story prepared for why I look like a demented circus clown.

"Adele," my mother says from the doorway of the bathroom. From the corner of my eye I can see that she's holding Meggie and smiling at her. I don't think she's looking at me. I keep staring in the mirror. She asks, "What are your plans for tonight?"

"Thetalentshow," I mumble.

"The what?"

My lips feel squishy. My toe throbs like the bass of a dance song. *Bam. Bam. Bam. Bam.* I wish I'd put a sock on it. Maybe my makeup will distract my mother from seeing my taped-up toes. But I still can't look at her. "The talent show. I'm going. With Cara. She's coming to pick me up."

"You're doing what with Cara?" my mother clarifies.

Apparently what I'm thinking and what I'm saying aren't aligning at the moment.

I bite my lip and then say slowly, "The talent show." I continue staring at my face in the mirror. I raise my eyebrows up and silently mouth a long "Wow."

My mother snaps, "Did you tell me you were going to this?"

I shake my head, and she exhales loudly. "What if I'd had to work late, Dell? Who would've watched Meggie?" I am given no time to respond because she turns and walks away. *Nice talking with you, Mother.*

I grab the edge of the counter and exhale agony into the sink. I'm doped-up and *still* in pain. Great, just great. Now that mom's home, hopping is out of the question. I'm going to have to limp around and stick with the stubbed-toe story. I take one small step away from the sink, and stars pop into my vision. I feel woozy.

Deep breaths.

I open the medicine cabinet, grab the bottle of Vicodin, and shove it into my front pocket. As I exit the bathroom I resume the least traumatic way of getting around—only putting pressure on my heel. It's a tricky way for a drugged-up fat girl to get around, but it beats the heck out of putting my full weight on the toe.

Whispering curses, I manage to wrestle on a sock. As I

sit heaving and sweating on the edge of my bed, I spy my Adidas slides in the corner. I get the best idea. I heel-hop over and pick them up. They'll totally work. I clutch them to my chest in a hug. The thought of squeezing my broken toe into a sneaker was making me want to chop it off with a butcher knife.

Slides on, I hear Cara's horn.

I check my reflection. I look like I'm ready to give a blow job in the alley or eat some brains. I hear the car horn again.

I'm hobbling down the hallway, when my mother is suddenly in front of me. "Oh my God, Dell!"

My eyebrows lift. "Relax, it's just makeup." I put my foot flat, and clawing pain makes me dig my fingernails into my palm.

Another honk blares from the parking lot, this one longer and more insistent. "I'm going." As nonchalantly as I can, I heel-walk to the door.

"Why are you limping?" my mother asks from behind me.

I turn only my head, unable to endure the pain of maneuvering my entire body around to face her. "Stubbed my toe on the sidewalk."

"Dell, you look ridiculous. Between the face paint and the slides with socks . . . come on."

"Thank you, Mother." I close my apartment door and slowly take the steps down one at a time.

Floating in a Padded Bubble

"HOLY EFFING SHIT!" CARA SHRIEKS.

I close the car door. "You said heavy makeup. So sue me for being a good listener."

"What did you say?" She eyes me up and down. Apparently I am only still making sense to myself right now.

I shrug and do my best to fasten my seat belt. Getting part A into part B is hard when your eyes won't stay open.

"What are you wearing?"

"Comfort." I finally click my seat belt. I stare out the windshield, trying to ignore that Cara is glaring at me like a lunatic. She's not moving.

I give in and look at her. "Let's go," I say. Seeing her face makes me realize that she's right—I've overdone it. Embarrassment isn't the feeling I was hoping to experience. I feel so stupid. Cara's dress is purple and pretty, and she has stockings on with heels. I look like I'm ready to mow the lawn.

"Are you drunk?" she asks.

"No." I leave out the part about swallowing three Vicodin.

"You're acting weird. Are you still mad at me or something?"

At the moment, my anger floats in a padded bubble, its spikes no longer poised to slice and stab. "Thanksforpickingmeup," I mumble, ignoring her question. I'm doing my best to keep my breathing steady. I still don't know how I made it into this car without passing out. "Thankyouthankyouthankyou, Cara." I want my best friend to know how much I appreciate her driving me.

"I can't understand what you're saying, Dell." Cara starts the car.

Since my mouth isn't working, I stop talking. We drive to school in silence. I trace the pill-bottle bulge in my pocket with my fingers. Over and over again. Cara pulls up in front of the auditorium doors. I wipe my palms on my jeans and smack my thighs a few times to get me going. Somehow I've gotta get out of this car without falling over or puking on the sidewalk. Cara is already out and at my door. "Let me help you."

She certainly is Miss Helpy-Pants today. First telling Mr. Drueller to come talk to me, and now assisting me out of the car. If she really wanted to help me, she would produce a spare wheelchair or a pair of crutches. "I'm good." I steady myself as I gingerly stand. I slam the car door.

Cara's back behind the wheel in a flash. She leans down and says through the open passenger window, "I've gotta park. Meet you in there?"

I give her an a-okay. My trek to the auditorium is a slow go, but I make it. I'm sitting in the last row, wheezing like an old lady, when Cara, in her purple glory, shows up. I endure about ten thousand questions and comments from her as we walk down the aisle. Her last one is a whiny "Why didn't we go shopping for youuuu?"

I shrug. No one cares how the fat girl looks. I. Am. Invisible. No one will see me. They'll hear me—but no one will be able to remember what I'm wearing onstage. Period. End of story. Good night. The end. I pucker my lips to blow Cara a kiss. The stars are back, and I feel queasy. I never ate dinner. I shake my head in amazement. Me not eating is equal to the tides not coming in. Unheard of.

"You're as white as a ghost, Dell," Cara says.

"I'm hungry."

"Maybe they'll have snacks backstage. Come on, hold on to my arm."

I do, and it's 50 percent easier to heel-walk while holding on to her. Cara sits me in a chair backstage. It's a small space where the performers usually stand and wait before going on. It's got a door that opens to the hallway near the main office. There's a similar space on the other side of the stage. From where I'm sitting I'll be able to watch acts as they perform.

"I'll tell Mrs. Salvatore you have to stay here because of your toe. Don't go anywhere."

I can only nod. The wall and curtain swirl together, a jumble of tan and red. So pretty. I grin.

I lean my head back and close my eyes for a while. I startle as two cheerleaders come through the door. One is Brandon's beautiful sister, with her creamy skin, bright blue eyes, and black hair. They stand in front of me like frozen statues. I look them up and down. They're decked out in full cheerleading gear.

They whisper back and forth, and I hear the other one say, "You ask her, Kim." Then she nudges Brandon's sister. They look at each other with bulging eyes.

"Boo!" I say. They jump. I pull my foot back for protection because it's a tight space. "Ask me what?"

"Where do we go?" one whispers. I'm not even sure which one said it.

"Out there, I guess." I raise my hand to point, and it feels like my bones have disintegrated. My arm flops onto my lap. I want them to leave. "Goaway," I mumble softly.

Kim tilts her head a little and looks at my face. I can tell she's admiring my stunning makeup application.

They both snicker as they back out into the hallway. The door hisses shut, and I overhear Kim say—obviously loud enough for my benefit—"Taryn was right; she is a fat bitch."

Super.

Do Something Stupid

"DELL, THIS IS ALL I COULD FIND." CARA'S IN FRONT of me now, holding out a candy bar and a can of soda. "There's nothing back here to eat. I got Mrs. Salvatore to open the teacher's lounge so I could get these from their vending machines."

"Thanks." Perfect for my "diet." I grab both and crack open the soda.

"Here's ibuprofen for your toe. I got them from Melissa." She places them in my open palm.

I don't tell her I've already taken the Vicodin. Or that she kind of has two heads right now. I snort and giggle and wash down the pills with a sweet, fizzy gulp of soda.

Cara pulls the curtain aside and peeks out. "A lot of people are out there already. Do you want my mom to save your parents seats?"

I turn my head and pretend to be extremely interested in the stage crew kids working on the microphones. "Not coming," I say nonchalantly.

Cara drops the curtain and whips around. "Didn't you tell them you were singing? What do you mean they're not coming? I swear to God you seem wasted right now."

I lick my lips and taste some leftover soda. I love soda. Why is Cara flipping out? Doesn't she know that my parents are both fucked-up, so lost in their own worlds of misery that they wouldn't care if I blew myself to bits onstage. "Not sure what *you* mean."

"Are we doing this right now? Are we?"

"You have four eyes."

Cara leans down so we're practically nose-to-nose. "You *are* drunk!"

Mrs. Salvatore walks in on our little "moment." I catch a quick flinch when she looks me in the eye. I think my makeup startled her. "Dell, I have no problem with you sitting here during the show." She riffles through papers on her clipboard, then she smiles at me. "I just ask for no movement and no sound."

K. M. Walton

I nod.

She writes something. "Will you be all right waiting until the end to sing? Do you need me to shuffle things around?"

"I'm last?" *Since when am I last?* I was never last in rehearsals. They always have the best performer close the talent show. "What about Semih?" His violin performance was insanely good.

"Broke his arm skateboarding about two hours ago. His mother called from the ER."

The irony of this is not lost on me, despite the fact that I can't focus my eyes. One broken bone is being replaced by another. I burst out laughing. Both Cara and Mrs. Salvatore are clearly confused by my inappropriate response to Semih's broken-arm story. I breathe through my nose to silence the other giggle trying to escape. "Sorry," I whisper. "Not funny. It's not funny. But 'nother gimp is taking his place. S'kinda funny."

Cara gives me the evil eye. "Dell's had a long week. She's tired, Mrs. Salvatore."

Mrs. Salvatore says, "Right. Well, you're closing the show now. Blow them away, Dell. Just like in rehearsals."

"Exactly," Cara says. She crosses her arms and uses her eyes to plead with me. When Mrs. Salvatore is out of earshot, she leans down and whispers, "Holy shit, Dell. How are you going to sing? What did you drink?"

I grunt and then laugh. "No drinkie. Some of Mommy's pills, Car-car." I like the sound of that. Maybe I'll start calling her Car-car. Maybe it will lasso her back to me and it can go back to being just the two of us. Cara likes nicknames. She called Emma "Em."

"Pills?" she hisses. "What pills?"

"Oh, Car-car. I only took three."

"Yeah, well, you've got to get yourself together, Dell. Everyone's out there. You can't—"

My laugh cuts her off, and soda shoots from my mouth. I couldn't be any more un-together. I am like scattered rabbit turds. Tiny little me-pellets everywhere.

"What is the matter with you? You got that on my dress! I am done. Done!" Cara stomps away.

I'm alone.

I never got to thank her for trying to be a hero and talking with Mr. Drueller. "Shit." I close my eyes and listen. The auditorium sounds like it's full now. Lots of people talking, a little kid squealing, someone hacking up a lung. All of a sudden, the lights dim and brighten a few times to signal that the show is about to start. I gaze down at my throbbing toe and wish I had something to rest it on. There's a box of ropes and an orange traffic cone in this dark nook. The traffic cone might work. I nod, agreeing with myself, and go to stand up.

Not good.

My one leg buckles—I forgot all my bones are gone—and I smash back onto the chair. Hard. It makes a loud noise, and I can feel the laughter barreling up my throat like a charging bull. Apparently my arms are still working, because they react and cover my mouth. I howl into my hands. Melissa's voice cuts through my laughter as she introduces the show and asks everyone to turn off their cell phones. No one comes to scold me about being so noisy, and I am pretty calm by the end of the first act.

When the curtain closes, my stomach suddenly grumbles. I feel faint, so I close my eyes again. Why did I take those ibuprofen? Now I'm nauseous. I put my energy into not vomiting. Even though I can't see them, I know the dance troupe is jiggling and thrusting on the stage.

Maybe a sip of soda will stop my stomach from churning. I reach down and grab the can. Across the way I can see a freshman pacing. He's next. I take a long swig. The bubbly sweetness slides down my throat. I have high hopes for this soda because in addition to stopping the nausea, I need a boost of energy to hop over to the corner and grab that traffic cone. I've gotta get my toe up. It couldn't possibly hurt any freaking more.

The audience erupts into applause. I go. I figure the clapping will drown out the sound if I crash to the floor in a dead faint. I hop the two steps to the cone, grab it, hop the two steps back, and plop into the chair.

Everything goes black. "Uh-oh," I whisper. I should've done that slower. It takes a few minutes for my eyes to work again.

The piano kid's classical piece fills the auditorium. With my head resting on the wall behind me, I listen. He's playing way better than at rehearsals. Good for him.

"Look at her, Sydney." Cara and Sydney stand in the doorway. "She took her mother's pills or something."

I chuckle and lift my foot. "For that. It's broken." I give them a big smile.

Sydney squats down next to me. "Could I have one?"

Cara playfully swats at her shoulder. "Syd! We have to help her."

"What? If it's that good, then I want one. I don't have to perform." She twists up her hair and then lets it fall back onto her shoulders.

I reach into my front pocket and am about to pull out the bottle of Vicodin when Cara says, "She's going to get up there and do something stupid."

Stupid? I'm not sharing anything with these two. I close my eyes and will them to leave. I don't want to hear either of their voices anymore.

Cara says, "I've gotta go. Mrs. Salvatore's going to kill me if I'm not ready to go on. Dell's, like, passed out anyway." Cara's heels *click-clack* as she walks down the hall.

I don't open my eyes because if I do, I'll cry. Sydney whispers in my ear, "Sorry about the cow drawing. Taryn made me do it. She was pretty mad about what you did to Brandon that night at the party." She stops talking and pulls away. I pretend that my eyelids are superglued shut.

"Please don't tell Taryn I told you. I felt really shitty about it. I-I tried to tell you that day in class. I went to Mr. Drueller and told him I was worried about you."

I squeeze my eyes shut tighter.

"I didn't tell Mr. Drueller anything about Brandon, Dell. I swear."

I swallow hard. Everyone believes Brandon's story. No one has bothered to ask for the truth. Is it *that* hard for people to consider the opposite happening—Brandon raping *me*?

And Cara never went to Mr. Drueller.

She's not worried about *me*, about how I feel, about our friendship.

Cara is worried I'll do something stupid onstage.

No one is worried about me.

Eating Electric Guitar Notes

SYDNEY AND HER REVELATIONS ARE LONG GONE.

I hate people right now. I'd like to barricade myself in this corner backstage. I could build another wall and install a lock and it would be my own little dark cave. I wouldn't mind putting a cot and TV in here. Well, as long as I could have some food delivered.

I lift my foot to rest it on the pointy part of the cone, but my tree trunk of a leg won't cooperate. My leg and foot slam to the ground, and I shriek in agony. A hand covers my mouth again, and I quickly realize it's my own. Lava-hot pain rips through my foot. The audience is still cheering for the last performance. I don't think anyone heard me.

Lying down has an urgent appeal to me. My eyes roam the space. There is not enough room.

I watch Darren and Ty do their magic act. Let's just say they're no David or Criss. They give a good go, though, and the audience claps. Then two girls butcher some love song. More clapping. Blah. Blah. Blah.

Even though the acts can all see me sitting over here, they don't acknowledge me. The show goes on. During a tap dancer's set, I have a brilliant idea and flip over the cone, giving me a much wider place to rest my calf. In theory. The problem is twofold now:

1. I still have to get my leg up.
2. It'll be like trying to balance my leg on the tip of an ice-cream cone.

But I have to relieve the pressure on my foot. My toe feels like it's going to explode. I don't know if toes can actually do that, but I'm not taking any chances. That would be gross.

I'm gross enough as it is.

Brandon's sister, Kim, and her friend are onstage with six other girls now, cheering their hearts out. *Rah. Rah. Barf.* I'm glad I'm in the dark because I'm giving them the finger and, oh, is it satisfying to flip those two off.

I put my hand down as the cheerleaders scurry off stage right. But Kim and her friend skip toward me, arm-in-arm, giggling. Before I have time to yank the cone out of the way, Kim trips over it.

Since the chipper skippers' arms were linked, they both go down. Hard. The fall breaks them apart, and one lies face-down, arms and legs spread. Kim ends up in a twisted fetal position. For a second, I wonder if the girl who face-planted is dead, but she pushes herself up onto her hands and knees and crawls to Kim. "Are you all right?"

Kim sits up and shakes her head. As her face turns toward the light from the illuminated EXIT sign above the door, I see blood.

Kim's cheek is bleeding.

"You're blee'ing," I say. That didn't come out right. My mouth refuses to form words. *How am I going to sing?*

The two girls yelp at the same time. I'm guessing they didn't know I was still sitting in the dark. How can you miss me? Seriously.

Kim reaches up and wipes her cheek, effectively smearing the blood. Now she looks like she's ready to head off into battle or tackle the quarterback. "Oh my God! I'm bleeding!" Kim says to me with pleading eyes as she stands up. "You put that cone there on purpose. Didn't you?" She holds a helping hand out to her friend. "I told you, Julia, Taryn said she's a fat bitch. So did Brandon."

Under my breath I say, "Your brother's a skinny asshole."

Both girls raise their eyebrows at me in shock. I don't give a rat's hiney what these two think. I hope they tell him what I said.

Word. For. Word.

I can hear Cara playing her jazzy tune on the piano, which means I'm on in one act. I wanted to prop up my foot, and that never happened. I wanted to clear my head, and that never happened. At this point I don't give a shit about anything. I just want it done and over with. And I want these two freshman bitches away from me.

"Come on, Julia," Kim says. She yanks her arm and pulls her toward the door. "Let's go find Brandon."

"Kim, Julia." I reach up and blow them a big exaggerated kiss. "Catch it. Give that to Brandon."

They push open the stage door, and Kim snarls over her shoulder, "You wish, you fat fuck." As the door closes, their cackles mix with the audience's applause. It reminds me of machine-gun fire from those stupid action movies. I can nearly feel the bullets whiz by my face.

The guitar kid is next. He plugs the cord into his amp and starts strumming. Ahhhh, this sound is luscious. So much better than bullets. Notes string together like colorful candy beads. My mouth opens. I want to chew on them.

Melissa thanks the guitar soloist. I stop chewing on his music and watch him unplug and grab his amp as the curtain closes.

Crap, I'm next.

If I hadn't been trying to eat electric guitar notes, maybe I'd be ready. I'm not.

I'm wasted.

Like a Demon Possessed

I'M SUPPOSED TO BE OUT ONSTAGE. I PRESS MY hands into my thighs and stand. I straighten up and lift my chin so I can breathe. I get my bum foot into position and heel-walk out of the darkness. When I'm five feet out onto the stage, the red velvet curtain slowly glides open.

I'm already messing this up.

I put every ounce of focus and energy into making it to the microphone stand. I should've dropped out of this show. I should've stayed home like the gods were telling me to. Each time I look at the distance to the mic, I cringe. I swear it's getting farther away, just like first base during my last softball game. I puff my cheeks up with air and then release it—I don't need to look any fatter than I already do.

Three more steps and I'm in front of the mic. It's a freaking miracle. I put my shoulders back and suck in air through my nose. The lights are blinding. I squint to find Mrs. Salvatore and her signal. She points, and then my music starts. I have a few seconds before I come in, so I use them to unclench my fists and try not to projectile vomit on the front row. My nerves are kicking the Vicodin's ass.

I open my mouth and sing. I sound kind of whispery and soft, and I don't like it. My mouth messes up the word "away," and it comes out "alay." But I keep singing.

It's just me and the music. It's like the audience is behind a wall of light. Maybe the pills are winning now. I feel different. I don't care what anyone out there thinks about me.

The next chorus comes, and I let it fly. I grab the stand like I'm in a music video. I go for it. I sway my hips, then dip down. I yank the microphone out of the holder and throw my head back. My voice rolls and booms and fills every corner of the room.

It fills all the empty space inside me.

Close to the end of the song, I shoot my arm straight up and spread my fingers as if sparks could explode from my fingertips. The music stops. There's silence.

K. M. Walton

I think I just blew everyone's minds. I know I've officially blown mine. I place the microphone back in the stand, and I swallow.

Like a bomb, the audience explodes into applause and cheers. It's the loudest roar of the night. I lean to the side and bow.

I did it! I can't believe I did it. I wish the stage crew would turn the lights down so I could see everyone's faces, but I can't see anything. I lean into the mic. "Thank you." I smile. The smile feels extraordinary. The clapping continues, and I bow again.

On my way up from my bow, I stop for a second. I strain to make sense of what I'm hearing. There it is again.

A *moo*.

Then another.

Shouts of, "Do it!" erupt from the back of the auditorium. Even over all the noise, I recognize one voice as Chase's.

Maybe he'd laugh. Chase always laughs. Maybe they'd all laugh. I can handle the laughter because I'm controlling it. I can decide if they laugh or not. I want to hear them laugh. I want everyone to laugh. I do. Maybe if I do it Brandon will laugh. I know he's out there somewhere. He has the best smile. I want him to smile at me. I want him to like me and be impressed by my voice. What if Brandon ran down the aisle and up the stairs and made out with me in front of everyone? What if he used this microphone to apologize to me and tell everyone that he lied about everything?

Why doesn't Brandon like me? He had sex with me. You're supposed to like someone to have sex with them. He must like me. . . . Doesn't he?

I want to hear laughter right now. Laughter will squash my pain. Like a bug.

"Just do it!" Cara shouts from the left. She's backstage, so the audience can't see her, but I can. *I* hear her loud and clear. I gaze at my Car-car in her perfect purpleness, with her hands on her hips, nodding at me, telling me to "Just do it," and I see that she's not really looking at me. She's looking through me.

I turn back to the audience. These people see me. They just cheered for me like I was famous. Brandon cheered for me. This auditorium needs more entertainment. I can do that. I can be a star for them. Maybe they'll love me.

I bring the microphone to my mouth again, spread my legs, and squat down into sumo position. The back of the auditorium goes nuts. My broken toe doesn't exist right now. It's just me and the mic and my adoring crowd.

Low and deep, the *moo* pours out of me like batter.

I grin into the white lights. Again I moo. Then I bow. I fumble trying to get the microphone back into the stand

K. M. Walton

and it ends up clattering across the stage. The feedback squeal makes the room go silent.

The stage lights go out and the houselights go on, and I can see the audience for the first time. Mrs. Salvatore looks like she's about to shit a coconut. They all do, actually. Someone in the back stands up and starts clapping. Slow claps. I squint through my tears to see who it is.

Brandon.

He cups his mouth and shouts a deadpan "Wooooh!"

Like I'm possessed, my arm raises, and my middle finger stands alone. A solitary tree trunk in the field.

I just flipped off Brandon Levitt in front of six hundred people, including my principal and all of my teachers. A fleeting sense of vindication passes through me like a shooting star, then it's over. I don't want to stand here anymore. I don't. I feel bare and stripped clean. And I'm crying.

I hobble off the stage. When I'm back in the darkness, I wipe my cheeks. My hands are covered in jet-black mascara. Great. I looked like a freak out there—mooing with raccoon eyes. *You're stupid, Adele!*

I spot the overturned traffic cone, and I want to throw it. I reach for it. I wing it onto the stage. It bounces end-to-end and lands on its side. The audience gasps as the curtain slowly closes.

The Light Is Gone

CARA RUNS ACROSS THE STAGE, LAUGHING. "OH MY God, Dell, you are so crazy. That was hilarious! Did you see—"

I cut her off. "Get me out of here."

"Relax, spaz. I know a secret way out."

Cara leads me behind the stage, and I take the stairs slowly. She uses her phone to light the way. It's pitch-black and it smells like wet basement.

"Can you switch arms? You're stopping my circulation," she says.

I release my death grip. "Sorry."

Her phone goes dark, and for a split second I can't see

anything. "Shit," she says. Then her little light is back.

She holds out her other arm, and I grab on. "We're close," she says. "The door's right up here."

I don't say anything as we make our way down the narrow hallway. My toe is trying to rip its way out of the sock, my stomach rumbles, and I have to pee.

"My car is back here."

I don't ask where "back here" is. I don't say thank-you for getting me out of there. I am mute. I give Cara a nod. The mooing ruined everything.

She pushes open a door, and I think we're still underground. There's a set of dirty concrete steps in front of us. A waft of trash hits my nose.

"We'll go slow," Cara says. "I can't believe you took all those pills. It could've been so much worse up there onstage. You sang pretty great for being trashed."

The door clicks closed behind us when we're on the steps.

"That door's never locked, you know. That's what Sydney told me," Cara babbles. "She said she and Chase snuck underneath the stage last weekend after Melissa's party and made out on the balcony prop from last year's *Romeo and Juliet*."

I am incapable of responding.

I hear crickets. We must be outside. We make it to the top step, and I look around. Big, dark green trash Dumpsters are to my right and left. I know where we are now—we're behind the school next to the cafeteria. No one ever parks here because it smells like shit.

Cara asks me to let go of her so she can text someone. She looks over at me with a huge smile. "Just got us invited to the after-party at Sydney's."

She thinks I'm capable of going to a party right now? I stare at her with wide eyes as we both get into the car.

"What? Come on, it'll be the perfect place for you to un-embarrass yourself. You know, save face. You did throw a freaking traffic cone across the stage, Dell. People are going to talk. Why not face it head-on? Besides, you sang great. Everyone loved your performance. I'll bet you'll get lots of compliments. Compliments are good, right? But first we'll have to fix your makeup. It's, like, all over your face." She starts the car and drives.

Cara, my only friend in the world, doesn't see me, know me, or understand me. This rips my heart apart, and my sadness smooshes the pieces into an unidentifiable mound. I'm spent. "I want to go home."

"Whatever, Dell."

She doesn't even argue with me.

The rest of the drive home is silent.

My head is a jumble of phrases and words: *fat fuck, darkness,*

K. M. Walton

don't tell Taryn, like I'm in a music video, fat bitch, do it, stay still,
zombie makeup, Vicodin, you wish, you fat fuck . . .

"We're here," Cara says, putting the car in park. "What are you going to do, go up there and sulk in your room?"

I shrug. Now would've been the perfect time to tell the old Cara—my best friend—the truth about Brandon, what he did to me and how he lied about it. But that friend is no more. This new Cara has moved on to bigger and better things. The truth wouldn't matter to her anyhow.

Using one finger, she fiddles with the keys dangling from the ignition. She sighs, filling the car with her irritation. "I don't know what to say."

"Me neither."

She abandons the keys and drums her fingers on the steering wheel. "Do you need help getting up the steps?"

I can tell I'm holding her up. "I can do it," I say with absolute finality.

"I don't know, Dell. I guess things'll be better in the morning." Cara smiles. "They usually are."

I can't return the smile. My mouth won't form that shape. Besides, with my smeared makeup, I know I look like a horror-movie murderer right now.

"I'll text you from the party, okay?"

I don't know how to tell Cara that I don't want texts from

the party, so I continue staring out the windshield. All of a sudden she kicks off her shoes and grabs them. "My freaking feet are killing me. These high heels are mini torture devices." She reaches over and squeezes my forearm. "You sounded amazing, Dell. Seriously amazing. Just remember that part."

I stare at her hand—the one that's squeezing my arm. Her purple glitter nail polish matches her dress. I don't even own a bottle of nail polish. Or anything purple, for that matter. I suck at being a girl.

I suck at being a person.

I suck.

I maneuver myself out of the car.

Cara shouts through her open window, "Let's go to the movies tomorrow!" As she drives away, my phone buzzes in my pocket. It's a text from Cara:

Just go to bed. Tomorrow = new day.

I shove my phone in my pocket. I'm not ready to go upstairs yet. I wanna sit out here in the velvety night. There are so many stars out tonight. I want to float among them, alone, weightless.

Floating.

I cringe as a shooting pain jets from my toe up my calf.

How the hell am I going to make it up more stairs? "Carefully, stupid," I answer myself out loud.

My phone buzzes again when I'm on the third step. I can't stop now or I'll never make it to the top. My bladder reminds me that it's full and still wants to be emptied, pronto. I squeeze my crotch with one hand and grasp the banister with the other.

On the seventh step, my bladder waits no more, and I pee my pants. Right there on the steps. Once I start peeing I can't stop. "Oh, shit, shit, shit!" My jeans are warm and wet.

I look down and see that the carpeting on the stairs is still dry. I pat my hips. "Good job," I tell my jeans. I'll bet a size-two girl wouldn't have had enough fabric to soak up her pee.

I still have three more steps to go. When I lift my leg, I groan. Apparently when pee soaks into size twenty-four jeans it doesn't stay warm for long.

My hand is on the doorknob when I hear the television. I close my eyes and shake my head. I failed to consider that my mother would still be awake. I look at my watch. It's only ten forty. She never misses the eleven o'clock news. Holy effing hell. How am I going to hobble into the apartment, covered in pee, with black makeup smudged all over my face, without her seeing me? The sofa faces the damn door.

I decide to just walk in, head lowered, and limp down the hallway to the bathroom as fast as I can. I'll lock the door and jump in the shower before the questions come. I'll pretend I can't hear Mom knocking.

Before the ten million things that could go wrong with this plan start taunting me, I unlock the door and do it.

I make it, and I'm locked in the bathroom, panting as if I ran home from school. I put my ear to the door. I don't hear anything but the TV. Maybe Mom will wait till I'm out of here. Maybe the sleep gods have given me a gift and she's snoring on the sofa.

I look in the mirror. "Fuhh—" I can't even finish the curse. It looks like I've smeared my face with tar and dirt and blood. Everything's smudged. The rainbow eye shadow. The maroon lips.

Ugly. Smeared. Hideous.

I lean in so my nose is touching the mirror.

I want to see me.

My knees give way a little. The light is gone. My eyes are dark.

I see no one.

K. M. Walton

Gasping for Air

I DON'T KNOW IF I'VE EVER SEEN ANYTHING SO ugly in my life. My hair is matted on one side and a sweaty strand is stuck to my neck like a brown snake.

With trembling hands, I get undressed. I pile my pee-soaked underwear and jeans in the corner and lay my phone on the counter. I carefully strip off one sock and then the other. My toe is navy blue and black. The clear tape has rolled up on the side and my toe has swelled out around it.

Hot water. That's what I want. Hot water. I want to wash everything off me. The pee. The shame. The humiliation. The hatred. I climb over the side of the tub, using both hands to keep steady. The hot water runs down my body, and I put my head back so it hits my face. Black streams of water roll down my boobs as the mascara washes away. It's not hot enough. I reach back and twist down the cold knob. Steam fills the room, and I breathe in deeply.

Still not hot enough.

I turn off the cold water completely. I want my skin to bubble and peel off. I want my blood to go down the drain. I want to be a pile of sparkly clean bones, white and pure. No organs or tendons. No squishy brain. No broken heart. Just bones. Scrubbed of weakness.

After a few minutes of standing trancelike under the water, I snap out of it. I grab the bar of soap and lather every inch of me in my best effort to feel clean, to wash all the pain away. But bubbles and hot water don't have that power.

When I can't see my hand in front of my face, I figure it's time to get out of the shower. The fan has never worked since we moved in. Meggie always says it's like a cloud after I shower. She'd flip out and clap her little hands if she saw how thick the "cloud" is right now.

I can't believe my mother didn't even turn off the television, say hello, or check on me. I wish I could spend the night in the bathroom so I wouldn't have to face her. But I hardly fit in the tub standing.

I get dry and use the towel to wipe off the mirror. I lean in and inspect my face. I still have eyeliner underneath my eyes. "Wow, what is that stuff made of?" After multiple swipes with a tissue my face is finally makeup-free.

Ugly with makeup. Ugly without makeup.

I gather my clothes into a ball underneath my arm and grab my phone. I clutch my towel and open the door quietly. I look down the hall. Mom doesn't appear.

I make it to my room, and my phone buzzes in my hand. I've got another text from Cara. I'll read it later. I put my phone on my nightstand, drop my dirty clothes into the hamper, and grab my pajamas and underwear from my drawer. After I'm dressed for bed, I watch Meggie asleep in her crib. My stomach reminds me that I'm starving. I know it's late and I should start my diet again. I should climb into bed. But my stomach would growl all night and wake—

Screw it.

I make my sandwiches in a dark kitchen. I'm too afraid to turn on the light. I try to eat like a ninja, straining to hear if I've woken up my mother after each bite. Each time the sandwich makes entry into my mouth, I repeat *I just can't believe it* in my head. I remain shocked by Sydney's confusing behavior. She was the one who taped the cow picture to my locker. But it was also Sydney who told the counselor she was worried about me. I don't even know Sydney.

Cara should've gone to the counselor, paralyzed with concern for her best friend, Dell. It should've been Cara.

Maybe Cara and I never really appreciated each other. I should've told her how I feel, really opened up to her.

I listen to the fridge hum. A shitty thought cuts through the droning: I don't know how to talk about things that really matter. Maybe that's why I'm a size twenty-four. I am full of problems. Stuffed like the trash cans after last lunch. Each fat roll is swollen with unresolved issues I should've let go . . . or talked about. I keep it all inside, every bit of it—the confusion of my parents' divorce, the resulting broken heart, the disappointment of my father, my mother, my best friend. The rape.

I don't know how to talk about my life with anyone. Self-doubt and hatred, two obnoxious assholes, are the loudest voices in my head. They're aggressive, bossing me around, intimidating me into silence.

As I swallow my last mouthful, I feel unsatisfied. I eye up the crumbs on my plate. Tears suddenly well up and roll down my cheeks. My eyes dart around the room as I swallow a sob. I rake my hand through my wet hair.

Food can't even satisfy me anymore. It disappears in the quicksand of pain.

I peek into the living room, expecting to see my sleeping

mother. She's not on the sofa. I lean in farther and strain to see if she fell off of the sofa or something. Where the hell is she? The bathroom? No, I would've seen her walk by.

I go over and turn off the TV. I limp back into the kitchen and turn on the light. That's when I see the note taped to the cabinet.

I signed up for outpatient rehab. Starts Monday.

~ Mom

Outpatient rehab? I stare at the words and read them a few times. My eighth-grade health teacher said that admitting you have a problem is the first step to recovery. Or something like that. Maybe my old mother will re-emerge from her drug-induced stupor. The mother who listened and smiled and tucked me into bed with kisses. I bet Meggie will prefer clean mommy to drugged-up mommy. Meggie deserves better, so if signing up for outpatient rehab will allow clean mommy to come home, then bring it on.

I grab two ice-cream bars on my way past the freezer. Each bite I take as I make my way down the hallway is followed by a cringe—my toe is still killing me. A huge chunk of chocolate coating nearly falls to the floor, but my mouth saves the day. I'm enjoying the rich chocolate melting and gliding over my tongue when I see that my mother's door is closed. I try and remember if her door was closed when I walked past earlier. She was probably in her room the whole time. I can't believe she just went to bed without making sure I was home safe.

I sit on the edge of my bed and eat the second bar. Outpatient rehab. Huh. I think that's where the drug addicts only visit for treatment. They don't live there. I forgot about that kind of rehab. I wonder if it'll work. Would she stay up to say good night to me like before? If my mom gets clean, will my father break off his engagement to Donna and come back?

I get myself into bed so I can elevate my toe. Even with three pillows stuffed behind my back I'm not comfortable. I reach over and put another pillow under my foot. That's a little better. But I'm not tired. I picture Brandon standing out in the audience, clapping. If he'd been closer I would've shoved him to the ground. I never did anything mean to him, yet he sought me out and lured me upstairs at Melissa's party like a pig to slaughter. He deserves the finger I gave him.

I'm probably going to be suspended for that bonus show I put on for everyone, which is good in a way, because I won't have to see any of those people for a few more days. My mom will most likely cry into her hands and tell me what a disappointment I've become. Then she'll complain that I wore a T-shirt and jeans onstage. I can't wait.

I grab my phone to read Cara's text that came in while I was gracefully peeing my pants.

> I'll put the pix my dad took
> up on FB later.

Pictures? Of me? I don't want to see pictures of me. I know I'll look enormous. The bright lights shining on my made-up face. Another text comes in.

> I KNOW u r awake.
> This party is killer.
> Go online. Pix r up.

Cara will text me all night until I look at the damn pictures. I sit up and rearrange the pillows. At one point my foot dangles off the side of the bed and blood surges into my toe. I think the pain pills are still working because it wasn't that bad. I lift my leg and gently elevate my foot again.

I tap the icon on my phone and read through my wall. Every post is a compliment on my singing. I read each one two or three times, but it all seems pointless. I scroll down and find the SHS Talent Show photos Cara posted.

The first photo is Cara in all of her perfect purpleness at the piano. Her dress looks pretty. Her hair looks pretty. She looks pretty. The eleven comments below the photo reflect my thinking exactly—they gush with hearts and exclamation points and smiley faces.

The next photo is Cara standing in front of the piano. She's beaming, blinding the audience with her smile. More admiration below. Fourteen comments. I want to add one of my own. I type out: You kicked ass, girlfriend! But I hit the backspace and erase it. Girlfriend? Who even says that? Plus, the exclamation point was too much. Too cheerful. I type out: You nailed it.

Erase.

Too blah.

I move on to the next photo. It's me. My hands are wrapped around the microphone stand, and I'm belting it out. My makeup actually doesn't look too bad; Cara was right. I squint and study the photo. Her father zoomed in, so my socks and slides aren't in the picture. Thank God. But my body is in the picture all right.

Shit. I am gigantic. I click back to Cara's smiling photo and then back to me. I am easily twice her size. Maybe more. She probably weighs a hundred and ten pounds after a big

K. M. Walton

meal. A few more clicks back and forth between the photos, and I zoom in on mine. That's when I notice the tag.

WHALE

Someone tagged me as WHALE. I stare at the word. Each capital letter punches me in the face. W-H-A-L-E.

I click to the next picture. Me again. It's an even tighter shot of my torso and head. With a trembling hand, I click to see if this one is tagged.

WHALE

The next one is of me smiling. Oh, I'm soaking in the applause, I can see it in my charcoal-lined eyes.

WHALE

I choke for air. How many more photos are on here? I click to the next. It's another one of Cara. I go back to my first photo and scroll down to the comments. Twenty-three comments. Holy shit. Holy shit. Holy shit.

My phone buzzes in my hand. It's another text from Cara. She's probably telling me not to look at the photos. Too late. I don't read her text. I go right for the comments.

The first comments are all compliments. They deteriorate at about the fourteenth. Unleash the evil.

Taryn: She's a mannish beast!!

Chase: mooooo, cow, mooooo. LMFAO

Taryn: Chaser, where ru guys & why am I not w/u? Tell Brandon to wait for me.

Chase: he's already wsted. me tooooooooo. Cara, go get whale, i want to lafffff.

Taryn: Even if she moos, Dell will always be a WHALE.

Leaving Craters

I DROP MY PHONE IN MY LAP.

Everyone can see that. *Everyone!*

I'm going to throw up. Broken toe or not, I fling my feet to the floor and hobble to my trash can. Everything comes out. I stand in the shadows and gag a few more times. "Oh my God," I whisper. I wipe the tears and spit from my face. I don't feel any better.

Meggie rustles in her crib. *Please don't wake up, please don't wake up,* I repeat silently. As much as I love my sister, I could not face her right now. Not with vomit on my breath and WHALE tattooed across my forehead.

My phone buzzes and lights up with a new text. It's gotta be Cara. I can't deal with her. I want to be alone. I want to sleep. I want to dream and dream. Bed. I want to get back in bed. I have to stop midway and regroup because I think I'm going to faint. I can't faint. I'd wake the neighborhood when I hit the carpet.

Deep breaths. In and out. That's it. Calm down. Three more steps and I'm sitting on the edge of my bed. I made it. I grab my phone. Cara has deleted the photos. The comments are gone.

Fury shatters everything underneath my skin. I feel liquefied, my rage overflows. Drowning me. I'm nearly under.

The truth. I have to tell everyone the truth—what really happened at that party.

Without hesitation, I type in a new status on my wall and hit enter: Brandon raped me.

I stare at the words, expecting to feel some kind of peace. Instead of relief, I want to throw my phone and smash it to smithereens. No one will believe me. I need more pain pills. I breathe through my nose like a bull to keep the volume down. How my sister isn't wide awake by now is beyond me. But she's still sound asleep. I give up elevating my toe and rock back and forth instead.

Shit builds in my mind like a pyramid. So many hideous blocks. So much ugly. I shake my head back and forth. Fast.

K. M. Walton

Faster. I want the pyramid of shit to tumble to the ground and leave craters. Holes in the earth. I reach up and claw at my hair. I want the pain out of me. No matter how hard I yank my hair, I can't get it out.

The weight of my skin is suffocating me. My hands have minds of their own and they pull my shirt up, revealing my dimpled, white fat rolls. They squeeze the fat. I want a knife so I can cut this heaviness off me. Then people would stop letting me down.

Then someone would love me.

I'm overpowered by the fat. I grab hold of the flab hanging from my arms and tug and pull. I scratch at my exposed skin, and it stings.

I flip over and yell into my pillow. It is about as satisfying as kicking the towel. I want to scream until I cough up blood, but I can't risk waking Maggie.

If I were a good person, I'd text Cara and thank her for taking down the pictures. But I don't care anymore. I told the truth in my post. Everyone can comment and laugh until their sides cave in.

Why can't people leave me alone?

I want to be left alone.

I want to disappear.

I want to die.

The Way Meggie Smells

I BLINK NERVOUSLY, LIKE SOMETHING'S IN MY EYE.
I repeat the four words.

I.

Want.

To.

Die.

I stop blinking. A little bit of agony releases. I think it
again, and a larger chunk of misery floats away. Dying would
make it all end.

Out of the blue, Anthony Baldino's dead body pops in
my head. Freshman year he sat next to me in math. He stole

his dad's truck and a bottle of vodka. He got shit-faced and crashed into the back of a bus. He was only fifteen.

His dead body is the only one I've ever seen. I remember his older brother getting escorted from the church during the funeral because he couldn't keep it together. Everyone talked about Anthony's death at school. The counselors gave special presentations. The teachers didn't assign homework for the first two weeks of school. Anthony's buddies had bright red passes from the principal to excuse them from class if they needed some time alone.

It was a big deal.

I don't want any of that crap. I want to die and not be missed. Or is that insane? I grip my sheets and squint. I want people to feel guilty. Specific people: Brandon, Taryn, Chase, Jacob the table-lifter, my old softball team, my father, DD. Even Cara. I want my fat face to haunt them when they go to sleep.

I want to sleep forever.

I look at the clock. It's almost one in the morning. I quiet my mind and ask myself one question: Do you really want to die? I let the question sit there, like a turkey on a platter. I don't repeat the question. One asking is sufficient. It's the king of questions. The pungent taste of vomit mixes with my spit as I swallow.

My answer is clear: I do.

I suddenly feel light, like a feather, a balloon, a bird.

Free.

This does not surprise me, this weightlessness. It simply feels right. Like something I've been waiting to experience, but I just didn't know it.

My sister moves in her crib. She can't see me dead. It would mess her up for life.

Will my killing myself ruin my mother? I get still and think hard on this one. I know she hates the clothes I wear, buying enough food to feed me, saving for my college education. And my weight.

She hates *me*.

If I go, then she won't be so anxious. She's going to outpatient rehab, so she'll be clean soon. Will she feel guilty? Maybe. I don't want her to feel guilty. If I word my suicide note right, maybe I'll be able to lessen her remorse. In time she could even be happy. She has Meggie.

Meggie's too little to understand. She'll be confused for a little while, but she'll be all right. She has my mother. They'll always be there for each other, I know that. Life will be much easier without me. Meggie will get a lot more attention, and she can have every penny of my college fund.

I can't believe how clearly I'm thinking right now. Everything

K. M. Walton

makes sense. I've never been so sure of anything. My heart quickens because if I'm doing this, I'm going to have to make some stuff happen. I have notes to write, pills to take, and—

Where can I go? I can't do it in the apartment. I don't want to die in my mother's car because she'd picture me every time she had to drive in it. I am out of ideas.

I pluck the prescription bottle from my damp jeans and pour the Vicodin onto my palm. Only five pills. Even with the three I've already taken I know that won't be enough. I'm a big girl. I hobble to the bathroom, open the medicine cabinet, and grab the first bottle I see. It has a little sticker on the side telling people they shouldn't operate heavy machinery. I dump the pills on top of the Vicodin. This should be good. I carefully rearrange the pill bottles on the shelf so they appear untouched.

I'm halfway to my room when I think, *Water—I'll need water.* I pause and tell myself I'll grab a water bottle on my way out once I figure out where I'm actually going to die.

Maybe I'll borrow my mother's car, drive to my father's apartment, and spread out on his front walkway. That way he and DD would be forced to step over me. My stupid father. I didn't even consider how my death will affect him. He'll probably cry some phony tears and then run off to the spa with DD to alleviate the stress and tension of my suicide.

I don't care what he thinks.

Cara will freak out. This I know. She'll be bummed. But she's got new girls who will hug her and pet her. She'll be fine. She's got college and sex and parties and husbands and children to look forward to. She will move on. She was ready to dump me as a friend anyway. This can work to her advantage, pushing her straight into the arms of new friends.

I yank my backpack onto my bed and grab a pen and my math notebook. Again I lift my bum leg and situate my pillows behind me. I need to write a suicide note. I jot on a fresh page:

Dear World,

Fuck off.

~Dell

I scribble it out.

Saying good-bye is hard. What the hell am I going to write? How do I put my feelings on paper? I suck at writing. I've never kept a journal. How will I compose decent suicide notes? I want to write one to Meggie, Cara, and my mother, and an eff-you to my father. Do people do that? Write more than one note?

I put the notebook and pen on my lap.

Tears roll down my cheeks as I think of random things I'll miss. I will never again taste chocolate melting on my tongue, hear the birds singing. I will never again feel my sister's little hand in mine. Never smell Meggie's perfect smell.

I wipe the tears from my face and stumble to her crib. I need to smell love right now. Meggie is facedown with her little butt in the air, and her blanket is in a twisted ball just next to her head. I carefully pick up her blanket, and inhale. Can I leave her? What if she needs me? What if she cries for me? Misses me? Can I do that to her?

WHALE

Too fat to play

Fat fuck

Held him down

WHALE

Each thought is a knife stabbing through the fat. Making fresh wounds. I can't face those people again. Even though I posted the truth, I know everyone at school will still believe I held Brandon down against his will and forced him to have sex with me. People will think I pursued him, coaxed him upstairs, and sat on him, practically squashing him while he begged me to stop.

I choke into Meggie's blanket to silence my sob.

Taryn Anderson believes Brandon's story because it's easier for her to accept. Her gorgeous, popular, boyfriend was nearly killed by beast Adele as she forced herself on him. There's no way she'd recover from the truth. That he flirted with me. Kissed me tenderly. And then held me down and raped me.

I've lost everything that matters to me. Softball, my family, my friend, my dignity, my dreams. The only things I'm full of are food and pain.

Someday my sister will understand. When she's my age and dealing with this mixed-up part of life, maybe my death will make sense to her. I have to believe that. I sniffle and wipe my nose. I've gotta stop blubbering and get moving.

I reach down and, with the lightest touch, rub her little back. Meggie doesn't stir. The tears gush from my eyes. Drip. Drip. Drip on the mattress. I bury my face in her blanket again. I inhale deeply and smile through my tears.

This smell is . . . heaven.

K. M. Walton

In Complete Darkness

I CURL UP ON MY BED WITH MY SISTER'S BLANKET across my face. I have to figure out where I'm going to die. I've visualized every possible location around my apartment complex, but none seems big enough for me to lie down.

I sit straight up in bed.

The blanket falls onto my lap. I know the place. Of course it's the place. My clock says it's close to three now, and I do not want the sun coming up until I'm gone. I've gotta hustle. My pajamas are replaced by a T-shirt and a fresh pair of jeans.

The thought of dying ignites me. It's like the Grim

Reaper has given me mouth-to-mouth, filling me up with a dark purpose. I am in control. A flood of peaceful excitement makes me smile. I'm happy now. I have maybe an hour or so to live, and I'm happier than I've been in two years. My fingertips tingle as I stroke Meggie's blanket. A sense of contentment crawls up my arms and settles in my heart.

I want to die.

I'm ready to let everything go and release it back into space. The bad and the good. I hope the crap energy evaporates. I don't want it to survive without me. But all the good must go to my little sister. I want every bit of my soul's residual goodness to land on Meggie like tiny sparkly feathers. Then I'll always be with her.

I somehow pull on a pair of socks and slip my feet into my slides. I'm dressed to die. This thought sends a fresh shiver of excitement up my spine. I'm doing this. My shit life will no longer be connected to me. I can float up with the stars. Weightless. Free. Happy. I dump my backpack onto my bed. I stare at my math textbook. I'll never have to do trig proofs again. I shove in the pills, my cell, and Meggie's blanket, then zip it shut.

I'm ready to write my letter now. I grab my pen and notebook and let it out.

Dear Mom,

All that matters is that you loved me the best way you knew how. Tell Meggie I love her. Tell Cara I'm sorry and that I was telling the truth. Tell Dad he's a motherfucking selfish asshole.

Please don't be mad at me for too long. This is not your fault.

I love you,

Adele

I quietly rip the page from my notebook and fold it in half. I'm close to the door when I realize that I want to take one last look at Meggie. I turn around and walk to her crib. Her butt's still in the air. This makes me smile.

I whisper, "Bye, baby girl. I will always love you. Be good to Mommy. I'm sor—" I choke. The rest of my words will never leave my throat. I have to go now.

I stand at my mother's closed door and lightly put my open hand on it. I shut my eyes, let the tears roll down my cheeks, and create our good-bye. . . .

Mom, things will be all right. You'll see.

I understand, Adele. I love you.

I love you too.

I mouth "I'm sorry."

In the dark kitchen, I add a water bottle to my backpack and lay my letter on the table. I unfold it and flatten it out with my hands. I hate the frayed edges. It looks sloppy. I want it to look perfect. I carefully tear off the ugly part and then reflatten it.

When I'm satisfied, I grab my mother's car keys and limp out the door. I take a few long and drawn-out breaths before I start my trek down the stairs. I'm good. I can do this. I will never have to look at Brandon Levitt or Taryn Anderson again. They can have their beautiful, popular life, get married, get old. Then he'll get fat and lose his hair and she'll get stretch marks and a fat ass.

"Go to hell," I whisper to no one.

I make it to my mother's car, but I'm dripping sweat by the time I get there. As soon as I'm behind the wheel I have to wipe my hands on my jeans and mop off my face. I get the key in the ignition, and the car comes to life. Before any late-night nosy-bodies look out of their windows, I drive.

Not a single car passes me on the road. Every stoplight is blinking. I like feeling as if I'm the only person awake. It's fantastically peaceful. I roll down my window and let the cool air whoosh against my flushed face. I let the car idle at the STOP sign next to the softball field and stick my arm straight out my window and give it the finger. My cheek rests on my shoulder and I gaze at the dugout. It wasn't that my teammates never meshed with me—I never meshed with them. I never gave any of those girls a chance.

My foot releases the brake, and I slowly accelerate. I un-stiffen my middle finger and form a fist. I punch the top of my thigh with everything I've got. With gritted teeth I take the pain; the sting will have to count as my apology to my team.

I pull into the parking lot and drive around the back of school. Crap, I forgot about the lights. They're always on in this parking lot. *Doesn't matter,* I tell myself, *no one's here.*

As soon as I park the car, the smell of trash invades my nostrils. I make no move to roll up the window. Instead, I close my eyes and let filth and rot slide into my lungs, where they feel right at home with my decomposing heart.

My buzzing phone makes my eyes snap open. Cara is still at it. I unzip my backpack and am about to turn off my phone when I'm face-to-face with her latest text.

> We have to talk.
>
> I'll call u in morn.

I stare at her text and realize that I feel nothing. Cara will call me in the morning. I will not answer. I won't see her ever again, and I'm okay with this. I leave my phone on the front seat. I've gotta get in there. It's almost four o'clock.

I use the shoulders of my T-shirt to de-sweat my face again, then roll up the window. I grab my backpack.

Time to die.

I leave my mother's keys on the front seat and the car unlocked. I don't want her to have to pay some locksmith jerk to get them out. I don't slam the car door, but gently click it shut. The loud noise would break the tranquility.

The stairs down to the dark hallway underneath the stage are directly in front of me. I hope the door is unlocked like Cara said. I loop both arms through my backpack, like a five-year-old, and limp down the stairs. The metal doorknob is cold to the touch, and it turns all the way. Score.

I look over my shoulder with one last glance to make sure that I'm alone. I am. I push the door open, hop inside, and close it behind me.

I am in complete darkness.

"Ohhhh," I exhale. I have no phone. No flashlight.

K. M. Walton

How the hell am I going to make it to the stage? It's like construction-paper dark down here—thick and pulpy and heavy. I lean my head back and gently gong it on the door once, twice, three times. How could I have forgotten how dark it was down here?

I wait until my eyes adjust. After a minute or so I can actually see. Who needs a flashlight? I have good eyesight. I go slowly because I don't want to knock into anything and make any more noise than I already have. I don't know if the custodial staff works on Saturdays, but I think I'd freak out if one of them stopped me from doing what I came to do. Now that I've made my decision, I can't go back.

I can't go back—I don't *want* to go back.

The pills I took earlier dull my pain, so I quicken my pace. I reach the top of the stairs leading to the stage.

I ease the side door open and listen. I am alone. Only the red EXIT signs are illuminated, and compared to the darkness I just navigated, it seems as bright as day up here.

I make my way onto the stage and squint. *Where's my traffic cone?* I scan the space. Someone put it back in its original place. How nice. The curtain is still closed. I was hoping it would still be closed.

I stand in the exact spot where I sang and take off my backpack. What happened on this stage floods my brain, but I remain calm. I let each moment replay as I breathe in and out. I want to remember it all: the fizz of the soda on my lips, the blood trickling down Kim's cheek, the few seconds of stunned silence before the rush of applause. The mooing. The airborne traffic cone. All of it. Each instance proves I was alive, that I lived. I did exist on this planet, even if it was only for seventeen years. I was here.

Will I be remembered?

I roll my eyes. I don't care about that.

I try to sit down on the stage, and I cry out in pain. Toe still broken. Body still obese. I stand there, out of breath. If anyone is in this building there's no way they didn't hear me scream. I strain to listen for footsteps. All is silent.

I am not dying in a chair. I'd be slumped in some ugly position or fall flat on my face. I have to get down on the stage floor somehow. I want to lie down. I lift my one leg out in front of me and go into a squat. Gravity and fat girls are a lethal combination, because it feels as if someone pushes me. I slam onto my ass, and the back of my head smacks the stage. Hard.

"Ow. Shit. Ow." I reach back and check for blood. My hand is dry. At least I'm lying down now. My chest heaves as I get my bearings. I lift up on my elbows to locate my backpack. I must've kicked it across the stage by accident, because it's five feet away from me. God, my butt hurts. I went down hard. I roll over onto all fours and crawl to my backpack. Each time my hands make contact with the stage, I see white spots. I probably have a concussion. I crawl back to my spot, dragging my backpack.

I want to die where I sang. It's stupid, but it's what I want to do. This is the spot where I was the happiest. I'm hoping the wood floor has leftover energy—blissful energy—that will penetrate my skin and lift my soul from this world. Lift me up to the stars.

Even though I didn't put anything about it in my note, I know it won't take that long for people to find me. School will be filled on Monday, and my mother's car is out back. They'll look around in here.

I unzip my backpack. I wish magic was real. Gazing into David Blaine's or Criss Angel's eyes as they did their magic and made me vanish into thin air wouldn't be bad. I smirk. *Thin* air.

There aren't sexy magicians here. All I've got are pills.

I hold the pill bottle in one hand and the water in the other. I know I have to take every pill or it won't work. Some senior girl tried to kill herself with aspirin and allergy medication, but she didn't take enough of either and ended up with a pumped stomach and a bunch of finger-pointing and whispering.

I have to do it right.

Five pills down. I look up into the shadows of the stage lights above me. I'm relieved they're not on, because dying while cooking underneath hot lights like a convenience-store breakfast sandwich does not sound appealing to me. I sweat enough as it is. Five more. Deep breaths. Then another five. I inspect my water bottle—I don't have much left. Why didn't I grab two bottles? Stupid. I swallow more pills with less water, and one gets stuck in my throat. I gag a few times, and then it's down.

I look inside the pill container to count how many groups of five I have to take. I dump what's left onto my palm. I've got twelve more to go. Three more swallows. I lift the water bottle up to my face. I think I can do it. The first group goes down easy. The stage lights are so big up there. Five more. My stomach twists. Is it happening already? It can't be; they're capsules. I swallow the last two and marvel that I still have a sip of water left. I finish it and lie back on the stage.

I don't feel good.

I feel like I'm going to throw up. I can't do that or every-thing will be ruined. I left a note. I can't throw up. *Don't puke!* I shout in my head. I don't.

I close my eyes. I am relaxed. I want this. I imagine the stage suddenly shooting light from underneath me, microscopic particles of happiness releasing from the floor and penetrating my skin. Through my layers of fat, I feel it. I swear I can. A warm sensation tingles up my legs. Are the stage lights on now? My eyes droop. It's still dark. But I can feel the happiness. It's real.

I lie perfectly still for a while. The absolute silence is calming.

A sharp prickle starts in my fingertips and pulses with each heartbeat. I open and close my hands a few times, then rub the smooth, shellacked wooden floor beneath me. I can't feel anything. My hands are numb. I slowly lick my lips. Or do I? I can't tell.

Meggie! I forgot her blanket. I want it around my neck.

Shit. I don't feel good. I have lost all sense of time. It takes a tremendous amount of effort to pry my eyelids open. They form slits, but refuse to stay that way. I give in and just close them. I fish for my backpack, pulling it to my side. It's still unzipped. I fumble around. Where is it? How could I have forgotten to take out Meggie's blanket? Stupid. I can't find it. My stomach really hurts. I can't puke.

I love my sister.

I try to remember her smell. I can't do it. My eyes won't open. I love my sister. She smells so good. I love you, Meggie-bedeggie.

My sister smells like lo . . .

Author's Note

DEAR READER,

I did not write this book to sensationalize or shock. I intended Dell's story to serve as a window into her soul—the soul of a broken human being. I wanted you, precious reader, to feel the pain of the bullied, the neglected, the heartbroken, and the humiliated. I wanted you to experience the absolute power of hateful words—whether said or typed online. Words count.

To anyone out there feeling alone: You're never alone. There is always someone you can talk to.

To anyone being abused: Tell someone. There is help out there that can make it stop.

To anyone who has been raped: Don't make excuses like Dell. Tell someone. Today.

And to anyone feeling suicidal, I say this: Even though we've never met, I want you to stay alive.

Talk to someone. Today. And if you're not satisfied with their reaction or level of help, talk to someone else. There is someone out there who will be your advocate.

If you know or even suspect that someone is feeling

isolated or alone or suicidal, reach out to them. Ask if they are okay. Listen. Pay attention to their response. Look them in the eye. See them.

Validate them.

I sincerely hope Dell's story touched your heart.

K. M. Walton

Acknowledgments

TO TODD, CHRISTIAN, AND JACK, MY HUSBAND AND sons, a.k.a. the three loves of my life—thank you for loving me with absoluteness.

To my mom and my three younger sisters, who are my four best friends—I am blessed to call you family.

Much love and thanks to the rest of my family and friends. You make me believe in myself, and that's priceless.

Thank you to my first readers: Nikole Becker, Margie Pearse, Christina Lee, Kathleen Scoboria, and Elisa Ludwig. Your insight and feedback helped shape Dell's story, and I will be forever grateful.

To Sarah LaPolla and Annette Pollert, my agent and editor—I still pinch myself because I can't believe you two geniuses are not only in my life, but are *my* agent and editor. Seriously, it's been such a privilege to have you both in my corner. Thank you for your hard work and dedication to this novel.

Thank you to the entire Simon Pulse team for giving Dell a beating heart. You all helped bring her to life.

Thank you to Radiohead for writing the song, "Codex," and to Coldplay for writing the song "Paradise." I must've listened to those two songs a million times while writing *Empty*, and with each listen I put myself in Dell's shoes. In my mind, "Codex" is *for* her and "Paradise" is *about* her.

Thank you, reader, for choosing *Empty* from the stuffed shelves and inviting Dell into your life. I hope you never forget her story.